THE WATCHTOWER SECRET

BOOK 3 of OCTOBERS

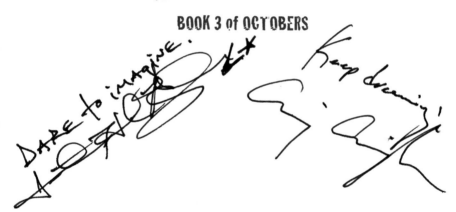

www.theoctobers.com

MOONSUNG
presents

THE WATCHTOWER SECRET
BOOK 3 of OCTOBERS

FROM THE IMAGINATIONS OF
J.H. REYNOLDS AND CRAIG CUNNINGHAM

ILLUSTRATIONS BY J.R. FLEMING

Dedicated to our creative luminaries,
who daily inspire us to become
better men and storytellers.

CONTENTS

In the town of Hobble, October never ends . . .

THE WATCHTOWER SECRET

BOOK 3 of OCTOBERS

31 Days Before . . .

Chapter 1:

Scares And Secrets

"I can't believe you forgot your marbles all the way back at the swamp," Scooter Scabbins said, pulling his straw hat low over his eyes. "Might as well leave them there for the night and we can go back and get 'em in the morning."

"It won't take any time at all. You're just being a scaredy-cat 'cause it's Hallows Eve," his twin sister, Stokely, taunted. She tightened the red bandana wrapped around her braid, and stuck her hands in her overalls pockets.

"*Me* a scaredy-cat? *You're* the girl," Scooter replied.

"You said it yourself," his sister retorted.

The eerie woodland leading to the swamp lay open before them like a black smile. In all their trips to the swamplands, they had never come at night. Everyone in Hobble knew strange things happened at the swamp at night, and that the Forbidden Watchtower at its far end was haunted. The swampland was the one place within the walls of Hobble the dozen Scabbins children were told never to enter.

Scooter hurried to catch up with his sister.

"It's not that I'm scared. It's just—something's not right in the woods tonight. I feel—I feel like someone's watching us," Scooter whispered. "Let's just go back in the morning."

"Oh come on, Scoot," Stokely proclaimed. "Honestly, what's the worst that could happen?"

Scooter glanced back across farmland that held thousands of pumpkins woven together by a network of fuzzy green vines. Earlier in the evening, he and Stokely had been asked to leave the Star Festival when they were caught sneaking crickets into the blueberry pies during the Junior Kyteboarding race.

"Alright, fine. But we're coming right back to the farm as soon as we get your stupid marbles," he insisted, then followed Stokely through the neighboring hay fields and into the woods.

As they neared the swamp, they heard voices carrying on the wind.

"Shh. You hear that?" Stokely asked, pushing through the trees. "Someone else is out here. Quick, hide!"

Right then, two large figures wandered through the forbidden woods. Scooter and Stokely crept from tree to tree so they would not be seen, and followed the duo deeper into the thicket until they arrived at the legendary Hobble Swamp.

A wooden sign with the word "*BEWARE*" creaked in the breeze. Mossy waters wove through small caves and around giant roots of blackened trees. A chorus of toads bellowed into the night, croaking atop lily pads and driftwood. The marshy swampland stretched all the way to the edge of Hobble, back to where the Forbidden Watchtower loomed.

The twins soon recognized the voices of Fink Karbunkle and Mayor Waddletub.

"I think it's safe to talk here," Mayor Waddletub whispered. "It's happened, Fink. The meteorite, the gatekeepers, the mark of the Vothlor, just exactly like it was at the beginning of the Old War. It's no surprise, after receiving word this morning that the Black Candle has gone missing."

"Hogwash! The *real* Vothlor were all destroyed years ago. You and I both know that better than anyone! Who reported the candle missing anyway? Shouldn't we be suspicious of the messenger before anyone else?" Fink questioned.

Fink had been Hobble's pumpkin farmer for fifty years before Gabbo Scabbins, the twins' father, was promoted to the coveted position.

"Tripper Boneglaze first reported the candle missing," Winky reluctantly admitted.

The Scabbins twins exchanged a curious glance at the mention of their favorite schoolteacher.

"But Tripper's far too young. Wasn't even born yet when the Ceremony Of Silence took place. How would he know anything about the candle?" Fink investigated.

"He knows for other reasons. Reasons I cannot speak of," Winky explained.

Fink kicked his boots into the dirt. "There ain't no

place for secrets in Hobble! Secrets already invited Malivar once, and I'll be blasted if I let it happen again. Tell me the plain truth of it, Winky. How did Tripper Boneglaze know about the Black Candle?"

Winky shook his head and replied, "I'm sorry, but I cannot tell you, Fink. Tripper's knowledge of the Black Candle is better left unexplained. Better for all of us, I assure you. Besides, all the other relics in the crypt were left undisturbed. The other secrets of Hobble's past remain protected."

"Then one of the Twelve must have spoken, and you're covering for them! There's no other way the candle could have been found! The secret was supposed to die with our generation, just as the Head Elder commanded! Taken to the grave!" Fink fumed. "Those who are seduced by the candle's power are led to do things they would not do otherwise. You know that I can attest to that more than anybody. I'm tired of your secrets, Waddletub. Secrets belong upon the gallows."

"All these years that I have defended your name, and now you call me the traitor," the mayor said coldly. "I brought you out here tonight to make sure that no matter what happens, you will not turn back into *his* service. I know Silas was a mentor to you. But I suspect you will soon be receiving a visit from Malivar, if you haven't already. I only hope that your loyalties have been tested for the last time. Beware of the Vothlor, Fink."

"Bah!" Fink sputtered. "You don't know a thing about my loyalties. And now, I don't know a thing about yours. Who stole the candle, Waddletub? Who was it? Why haven't you assembled the Council of Elders?"

Mayor Waddletub looked down at his pocketwatch. "I have to leave you now, Fink. There is something else I must do before this night is over."

Without saying a word, Winky waddled deeper into the forest.

"Maybe it's *your* loyalties that have changed, Waddletub!" Fink called. "Maybe they've even been *purchased!*"

Then he clenched his fists in anger and stalked off in the same direction as Winky.

Chapter 2:

The Forgotten Symbol

When the coast was clear, Stokely snuck through the woods towards the bank of the swamp. In the near distance, the Forbidden Watchtower rose out of the far side of the swamp like a crooked finger. A wicked moan bellowed from one of the open windows of the distant tower, sending chills down the twins' spines. Stokely looked ahead. There, in the glow of the moonlight, she could see her leather pouch of marbles lying on the bank.

"Safe and sound, right where I left them," she said, nudging her brother. "I'll be right back."

But just before she ran out from the covering of trees, a terrifying whisper invaded the silence.

"Myyy serrvant," the whisper called. "Sooon I will be resurrrrected."

Scooter reached for Stokely and pulled her back into the shadows of the trees. She tried to scream, but Scooter covered her mouth. They glanced at each other, and

Scooter put a finger to his lips.

"What in the name of Hobble was that?" Stokely whispered.

"I don't know," Scooter replied, suddenly feeling a bit woozy. "Where'd it come from?"

Stokely pointed out at the shoreline, right where her marbles lay. Only, no one was standing there. All they could see was a hazy, dark vapor hovering above the bank of the swamp.

The whisper continued, "Soooon you will be set freeee, and we will finishhh what we started. When the candle is lit, I wlll receive myyy cloak. And once I retuurrn, all Hobblers will wear the mark. Those who do not, shall die!"

The twins heard footsteps sloshing along the bank in the direction of the dark vapor. Then, as if by magic, the pouch of marbles lifted off the ground, and Scooter and Stokely could see them shimmering in the moonlight, held in the air by an invisible hand.

"Are you seein' what I'm seein'?" Stokely whispered.

Scooter's mouth fell open at the sight of it.

The footsteps started again, taking the pouch of marbles with them into the forest. But the Scabbins twins still saw no one—or no thing—attached to the sound of the footsteps. Only the strange haze. Then the steps began to trail away from the shoreline and back into the foggy woods.

When the sound of crunching leaves faded into the distance, Stokely jumped out from her hiding place behind the tree and ran to the swamp's edge. She stared at the place where her marbles had been, trying to think clearly.

"Scooter, if this is some kind of joke you're pullin', I

swear I'm gonna—"

"Stokely, you better take a look at this," Scooter called out in a trembling voice.

Stokely turned and peered down at the ground with a puzzled look.

Fresh footprints trailed down to the swamp from the woods, then doubled back up to the inner forests. Scooter crouched down and pointed. There, stamped into the heel of each footprint, was an unmistakable **V**.

Chapter 3:

The Man Who Lived Underground

Early the next morning at the fishing hole, Scooter and Stokely argued about whether or not they should tell someone what they had seen and heard.

"I tell ya, we have to find Sheriff, and tell Ma and Pa," Scooter said. "We can't mess around with this kind of stuff. I've never even seen Jypsi magic so powerful."

"Are you crazy?" Stokely argued. "If we tell what we saw, whoever or whatever that was will know it was us. My name's scratched into that marble pouch."

"Oh come off it," Scooter said. "We prolly ate too many jelly beans, and were just seein' crazy things."

"Let's visit the professor, then maybe we'll have more answers about what Winky and Fink were talking about."

The twins sloshed through the creek for half a mile until they arrived at a wooden door hidden away in the bank. A shallow porch jutted out from the doorstep, where a rocking chair squeaked beneath a dozen wind chimes. A rope dangling from the porch tickled the surface of the creek with its knotted end. The twins climbed the steep bank, gripping the rope, knot by knot. They slipped through the entanglement of roots and reached the front door.

Stokely knocked three times.

"Leave the talking to me," Scooter reminded his sister.

Stokely rolled her eyes.

Right then, an iron peephole opened, and a large brown eye looked down in surprise at the two young visitors.

"Howdy, Professor Boneglaze," Stokely greeted. "Me and Scooter need to ask you about something."

The peephole slammed shut, and Scooter and Stokely heard three bolts click open. Tripper Boneglaze opened his door, holding a flickering torch in one hand and the newest edition of the *Hobble Gazette* in the other. The schoolteacher wore cutoff trousers and a sleeveless, flannel shirt. His brown hair was trimmed short on the sides, but flowed curly all the way down his neck.

Tripper grinned at his two most mischievous students.

"School starts in half an hour, you know," Tripper said, eyeing the position of the sun over the twins' shoulders through the canopy lining Midnight Creek.

"This shouldn't take long," Scooter assured. "We didn't know who else to come to."

Tripper nodded and led the twins down a long earthen corridor, which ended in a cave-like den. A hearth fire blazed beneath a boiling cauldron in the far corner, illuminating the underground room with a dark red glow.

A small cot in the corner was held up by stacks of various library books.

"Anyone up for some hot cocoa?" Tripper asked as he planted the torch into the dirt wall. "I need some chocolate to loosen up my bones. Hobblers haven't been this frightened since the Old War."

Tripper tossed the *Gazette* to Stokely and walked to the stovetop.

"Strange times," Tripper continued as he shuffled for mugs in the cabinet. "Strange times, indeed."

The Scabbins twins eagerly scanned the headline on the front page.

GATEKEEPERS MURDERED!
MARK OF THE VOTHLOR HAS RE-APPEARED!
SHERIFF HOPSCOTCH HOT ON THE CASE!

Happy and Guffy are dead? Stokely wondered in shock. *And the mark of the Vothlor has re-appeared?!*

"I told you so," Stokely whispered to Scooter. "I knew what we saw was *real*."

A million thoughts and theories raced through their minds as they quickly leafed through the other headlines:

METEORITE FALLS IN TOWN SQUARE!
NO ONE CAN MOVE IT!

She suddenly stopped and placed a trembling finger on the final headline.

11

MAYOR WINKY WADDLETUB MISSING!
LAST SEEN IN TOWN SQUARE
JUST AFTER MIDNIGHT!

Scooter and Stokely glanced at one another.

"You think—Fink?" Scooter whispered.

Tripper returned from the stove with three steaming mugs of cocoa balanced on his arm. He handed the mugs to Scooter and Stokely and produced a handful of marshmallows from his pocket, which he sprinkled onto the creamy surface of the cocoa.

"So, what brings you to my end of the creek this morning?" Tripper asked.

"Just doing some fishing. And—" Stokely paused and looked over at her brother.

"And what?" Tripper asked, noting her hesitancy.

Scooter took a sip of cocoa and said, "Professor Boneglaze, we need you to be honest with us, like you always are at school." He paused and took a deep breath, then continued, "Have you ever heard of something called the Black Candle?"

Tripper squinted in puzzlement. "Black Candle? Can't say I have. But I've seen black candles before, if that's what you're asking. The Candletin has all sorts of colors for sale."

"No . . . no that's not what I mean. You don't know anything about an ancient Oath or a secret crypt?" Stokely persisted.

Tripper shook his head.

Scooter and Stokely exchanged a confused glance. Mayor Waddletub had said Tripper was the one who reported the candle missing.

"It's just—you see," Stokely faltered, feeling unsure. "Last night we heard and saw some things down at the swamp."

Tripper's grin faded into a look of grave concern.

"You shouldn't be exploring there," he scolded. "Things happen in that part of Hobble that no one should see. But—but what do you think you saw?"

Scooter fumbled for an answer, "We saw . . . We saw . . ."

"What he's trying to say is that we saw somebody who was invisible," Stokely interceded. "Or I guess it was more like a hazy smoke-shape. And we heard that *thing* whisperin' at the watchtower, and then it stole my marbles—"

Scooter elbowed his sister to stop her from revealing anything more.

"Oww!" Stokely yelped, and punched Scooter's arm.

Tripper's eyes widened in anticipation.

"Invisible?" he said, curiously. "Why, that's impossible. I'm sure it was one of your schoolmates playing a prank in revenge for all the ones you've played on them. Or maybe it was just a nightmare. Now, go on up to the schoolhouse and tell no one what you've seen—I mean, what you *think* you've seen."

When Tripper poured himself a second mug of cocoa, Scooter noticed his hand shaking, nervously. The schoolteacher then motioned the twins toward the door.

Scooter and Stokely stepped outside onto the precipice which overlooked the dark, rippling waters of Midnight Creek.

Tripper took a staggered breath, and pleaded, "For your

13

own sake, do not go looking for the dark vapor—or—or whatever it is! Forget whatever you think you saw. I don't want to see the two of you get hurt. Or worse."

"Yessir," Scooter said. "Thanks, Professor. We'll see you at school."

The twins turned to go.

"Just one more thing," Tripper said. "Did either of you happen to have any nightmares or see any other visions last night?"

Scooter shook his head, no.

But Stokely's brow furrowed as she thought back to the previous night. "Come to think of it, I did," she answered. "Hobble was on fire—and everyone was screaming."

Neither of the twins could explain the look of terror on Tripper's face.

Chapter 4:

Birthdays and Bewares

That evening, inside the Pumpkin House, the entire Scabbins family gathered around the massive kitchen table to celebrate the birthdays of the two eldest children.

Colorful balloons were tied to every chair, jack o' lanterns grinned from windowsills, and streamers were draped from one side of the house to the other. The rowdy Scabbins clan stood on their chairs as they serenaded Scooter and Stokely with the Hobble Birthday Song. Then Gabbo bellowed out a joyous whoop and slid two birthday cakes, fresh from Gubbles' Goodies, towards the end of the table, where Scooter and Stokely sat smiling at their family. Each twin wore a cone-shaped birthday hat with their initials stitched onto the front.

Gabbo lifted a mug of wassail above his head to make a toast.

"Here's to a dozen years down, and many dozens still to

come!" the farmer called out.

Fourteen mugs rose into the air and clinked against each other, spilling foam onto the checkered tablecloth.

Their mother, Rose, tossed handfuls of golden confetti into the air, and everyone blew kazoos while waiting for the birthday wishes to be declared.

Suddenly, a violent wind blew through the Pumpkin House, extinguishing every lantern and candle.

"Oh my stars," Rose whispered.

She pointed at the Hobble Tube in the den. It had come to life unexpectedly.

Gabbo lit a lantern on the tree-stump table and addressed the frightened children in a serious voice, "Gather around the Tube, little ones. This is probably just a little bit of nonsense."

The family migrated into the den, where they sat huddled together, entranced by the black-and-white buzz of the Hobble Tube.

Gabbo sat down on a stool and sipped his wassail, nervously, while Rose rocked baby Posy.

Principal Lilla Humplestock's face slowly formed upon the fuzzy screen.

The beautiful, silver-haired woman addressed the town in a calm, yet concerned, voice, "Fellow Hobblers, as you already know, two of our dearest Elders have been murdered, and our beloved mayor has gone missing. In order to protect ourselves during these dangerous times, I am hereby establishing a New Rule: no Hobblers are allowed outside the town walls *for any reason* unless they have a signed gate-pass from me. This is for your safety. I have also raised the Danger Flag to HIGH ALERT, and the watchtowers and Crescent Gates will be guarded around the clock. Do not worry. Do not fear. All will be set right."

The broadcast immediately repeated itself, and the Scabbins family watched it one more time. Finally, Gabbo stood from his chair and turned the round knob on the front of the Hobble Tube. The screen faded to black.

"What exactly does she mean, Pa?" Scooter questioned.

Gabbo thought quietly for a moment.

"She's just warnin' us to be careful, that's all. These times are no more dangerous than any other. Now, get ready for bed. We start planting the new crop of pumpkins in the mornin'!"

Rose glanced across the room at Gabbo, who had turned to look out the window at the gloomy pumpkin fields.

On her husband's face was a look she had never seen from him before. It was the look of *fear*.

At midnight, Stokely blew out the final lantern in the Pumpkin House.

All turned completely dark except for the dwindling firelight coals in the hearth. Hotchkiss, the family dog, lay curled in front of the dying fire. All the while, Gabbo's deep snores sawed through the silence of the house.

Stokely felt her way along the walls until she arrived at the ladder of the children's twelve-tiered bunk bed. As she climbed, she wished each of her brothers and sisters a goodnight.

"Goodnight Alice, Goodnight Apple, Goodnight Ferny, Goodnight Fart, Goodnight Mace, Goodnight Milky,

Goodnight Penny, Goodnight Posy, Goodnight Rip, Goodnight Rudd. 'Night Scoot."

"'Night, Stokely. And happy twelfth birthday," Scooter drowsily replied.

"It's not our birthday anymore. The coo-coo clock just struck midnight," Stokely corrected as she crawled into the bunk above Scooter's. "But happy birthday to you, too."

A moment of silence passed, and Scooter asked, "You think bein' twelve will be any different than bein' eleven?"

"Don't quite know," Stokely replied. "But they say twelve is a year of change, whatever that means."

Scooter took a deep breath, unsure if he wanted anything to change.

"I think it'll be a good year. The best yet, in fact," he replied, as if to convince himself. "Well, goodnight."

"Goodnight," Stokely returned.

She turned on her side and looked out the window across the pumpkin fields. A raggedy clan of scarecrows swayed in the October wind. Stokely was about to drift to sleep when she noticed a strange flicker of light in the far distance.

The light was coming from the Forbidden Watchtower beyond the swamp. Stokely bolted upright in her bunk.

"Scooter," Stokely whispered.

"I'm trying to sleep," Scooter grumbled. "Remember, we have to plant the new crop at sunup. And we have a dozen deliveries to make."

Stokely hung her head upside down and peered into Scooter's bunk.

"Just take a look out the window towards the Forbidden Watchtower. You see what I see?"

Scooter rolled over to face the window.

"What—What is that?" he asked.

Scooter and Stokely lay still and quiet for a moment before Stokely finally commanded, "Put your boots on. There's only one way to find out."

Chapter 5:

The Fink Karbunkle Conspiracy

The night was crisp and cool as Scooter and Stokely raced across the fields, leaping over jack o' lanterns and darting around the wagons which lay scattered across the vast farmland.

Up ahead, the light still glowed atop the Forbidden Watchtower.

"Mayor Humplestock mentioned something on the Hobble Tube about sending guards to all the watchtowers. Maybe it's just one of them making sure everything is alright on this side of town," Stokely suggested as they crossed the nearby hay fields.

"I doubt anyone's brave enough to go out to the Forbidden Watchtower. Everyone knows it's been haunted for years," Scooter replied.

Stokely stepped into the thorny thicket of vines and brambles, too stubborn to admit the overwhelming fear which brewed within her. She looked back at Scooter, who hesitated at the edge of the forest.

"Don't be a yellow-belly, Scooter," Stokely taunted.

Reluctantly, Scooter followed his sister.

"Murdered gatekeepers. A missing mayor. The mark of the ⚡," Scooter muttered. "And I don't think it's a coincidence that we saw Fink Karbunkle just before we saw the mark."

Stokely pushed through the thicket in determined silence.

"The Karbunkle conspiracy is just a story made up to scare kids like you."

"Nuh-uh! Fink was a member of the Vothlor, sure as I'm standing here. They say he murdered a bunch of kids at the end of the Old War with a hatchet," Scooter continued. "And who knows? Maybe Fink's somewhere nearby right now. Watching. Waiting with his hatchet. For us."

A thousand terrible whispers blew on the autumn wind, as if the Dead had been stirred by the mere utterance of Fink's name.

"Your spook stories ain't gonna work," Stokely finally said. "I already know that the trial proved Fink was purified, no longer infected with the vapor."

"Don't matter what the verdict was. Everyone knows they just didn't have enough evidence to send him to the gallows. But he was a Vothlor, alright. He had the mark. And now all this starts happening, and Fink just happens to be at the swamp with the mayor, who's now gone missing."

Footsteps crunched in the leaves behind them, somewhere in the deep darkness. A flood of fear washed over Scooter.

"We're being followed," Scooter whispered. "Someone's watching us."

"It's just the wind," Stokely replied.

Scooter checked over both his shoulders. Once he felt safe again, he continued his story, "I read that when the Old War started, Fink was a deacon over at the Ministry Of Light. It said if he wasn't farming pumpkins, he was at the Ministry, always working with the Director to get new members. But somethin' went sour. Once everybody started choosin' sides, the Ministry shut down. Don't know why. But they say Fink and that Director both received the mark

of the 𝖵, and betrayed everyone in Hobble. Course, at the end of the war, Fink was let off the hook because they say the things he did, he didn't really do—that his body was possessed by the dark vapor, and that it wasn't really him that was doing them. They said he was sorry for it all. But hardly anybody believed him."

The twins stepped out of the woods and headed into the dreary swampland.

"But even if all that's true, it happened fifty years ago," Stokely pointed out as she stared out over the green channels of swamp water. "People can change, Scoot."

"Not if you've got it in you to kill children. Once you're poisoned that bad, you're always poisoned," Scooter insisted.

But when Stokely looked out at the Forbidden Watchtower, the flickering light was no longer there.

Scooter pointed his shaking finger to the other side of the swamp, where a lantern swayed back and forth at the hull of a rowboat gliding through the thick fog.

"It's coming this way! Hurry and hide!" Stokely yelped.

The twins hid behind the trunk of an enormous cypress tree at the edge of the swamp and watched as the small rowboat crept through the greenish fog, slowly floating towards the shore.

"Who is it?" Scooter whispered.

"Can't tell yet," Stokely replied. "Fog's too thick. Probably the watchtower guard."

Two oars dipped into the waters on each side of the boat and propelled the vessel closer to the shore. Scooter and Stokely heard the creaking lantern swinging back and forth as the nose of the boat pierced through the swirling fog.

When the skiff was only a dozen feet away from them, the twins peeked around the tree to view the rower of the boat.

But the boat was empty.

Chapter 6:

A Contest For The Fittest

Early the next morning, Fink Karbunkle sat by the cackling fire in his retirement cottage, eating a bowl of cinnamon oatmeal.

The crabby old man leaned back in his rocking chair and admired his collection of polished trophies and plaques lined up along the fireplace mantel. Shiny ribbons, golden certificates, and countless framed articles from the *Hobble Gazette* hung upon the orange walls of the small cottage—all in honor of Fink's outstanding accomplishments during his decades as Hobble's most esteemed pumpkin farmer. The old miser's fingers itched to sink themselves into the fertile soil, to do what he loved most—plant and harvest pumpkins.

"If *only* I were younger," Fink sighed. "I'd run that rascal Gabbo Scabbins out of business—and right out of Hobble!"

Fink took out the morning's edition of the *Hobble*

Gazette, and spread it out on the breakfast table. He read with particular interest the report of the fallen meteorite, and the article about the missing paperboy, Red Crisp. As far as Fink could remember, it was the first time a child had been reported missing in Hobble in many years.

But when Fink read the headline on the third page, he spit his oatmeal across the room.

EDITOR'S CHOICE AWARD FOR
GREATEST PUMPKIN FARMERS IN
HOBBLE HISTORY
BY RINKY PINKERCUP:
1. GABBO SCABBINS
2. SEAMUS CRITCHFIELD
3. FINK KARBUNKLE

Fink slammed the newspaper down on the table and reached for his muddy boots, which hung from a nail by the back door. He could not believe that Rinky Pinkercup had published such a slanderous lie.

"It's time to put an end to Gabbo Scabbins reign over my legacy once and for all!" Fink shouted on his way out the door.

G abbo Scabbins bent down on one knee and placed his palm on the soft soil of the pumpkin fields, saying hello to the tiny seeds which he and his family had planted the day before. All of the Scabbins children were scattered across the fields, each of them with a tool or a sack of seed in hand.

They were about to break for their midmorning swim in Midnight Creek, when they saw Fink Karbunkle storming across the farm, angry as a hornet. The pot-bellied old man clenched the morning's *Gazette* in one hand and his golden lifetime achievement trophy in the other.

"You listen to me, Gabbo Scabbins!" Fink yelled through the chilly dawn air.

Gabbo arose from the ground and rested his hands on his hips.

"What's the occasion, Fink?" Gabbo asked.

"Maybe you can explain this rubbish!" Fink demanded. He pushed the *Gazette* against Gabbo's brawny chest, and waited while the farmer read the headline on the third page, which Fink had circled in red ink.

When Gabbo finished, he looked up at the old man and calmly said, "I'm not the one who wrote this, Fink. Maybe you should be talking it over with Rinky Pinkercup instead of wasting my time."

"Why, I oughta—" Fink shook his fist at Gabbo.

Stokely stepped in between Fink and Gabbo in order to protect her father.

"That proves my Pa is the greatest, and you're just a third place nobody!" she declared.

The other Scabbins children cheered at Stokely's proclamation, and threw handfuls of soil at Fink.

"Mind your tongue, you little grubworm, or you'll get what's coming to you!" Fink sputtered. He turned back to Gabbo, and bellowed, "I hereby challenge you to a pumpkin growing contest starting next October! A contest for only the fittest. Whoever wins the Century Award is the greatest pumpkin farmer who's ever lived!"

Gabbo pondered for a moment, and replied, "Fair enough. I'll be glad to put an end to this nonsense!"

Fink shook Gabbo's hand and stomped back towards his cottage on the western side of Hobble.

And thus, the grand contest had begun.

The Scabbins children whistled and cheered in support of their father. But a look of fear darkened Rose's usually cheery face.

She walked to Gabbo's side and whispered in a gentle, yet concerned voice, "Be careful Gabbo. I've never liked that man, or believed a word he said. He took the mark during the Old War. I'll never respect a man who would betray his own town—even if he is sorry for what he did."

"Now, Rose," Gabbo consoled. "The trial proved him innocent of the crime."

"Yes, but the blood was on *his* hatchet—and that's enough for me. I don't care if he says he was possessed by the dark vapor and that's what made him do it. I just hope Winky and that missing Crisp boy are safe. Worries me so."

"Hey Pa?" Stokely asked, hesitantly.

Gabbo looked down and patted Stokely's head. "Yes, my pumpkin pie?"

"Is it *really* true that Fink murdered a bunch of kids at the end of the Old War?" she asked.

Scooter joined his sister's side, anxious to hear Gabbo's reply.

"It's not my place to say what's true and what isn't," their father explained. "Some things are best left alone, especially after so much time has passed."

"Well, is it true he followed the Old Director of the Ministry right over to the side the Vothlor?" Scooter asked.

Gabbo began to nod, then stopped himself. "It's a complicated story, son."

Chapter 7:

A Meeting Of Elders

That evening, Fink stepped out of his cottage and stopped to feel the crisp, October breeze brush against his face, just as he had often done as a boy. The western neighborhoods of Hobble were silent as a ghost's breath. No chimneys puffed smoke into the starworld above, and no fiddles or checker matches enlivened lantern-lit porches.

Nearby, Huff Howler and a gang of kids, including Hoot Cricklewood, snuck towards the Crescent Gates with a boxlite in hand.

"Foolish kids. Playin' Goblinlight at a time like this! Get themselves killed, they will," Fink mumbled.

He bolted the door, tightened his heavy, wool overcoat, then vanished into the shadows of the nearby trees.

Once Fink was out of sight, Stokely and Scooter dropped down from the tree outside his house.

"Wonder where he's off to in such a hurry," Scooter whispered.

Stokely shrugged her shoulders.

"Prolly goin' to kill some kids. Come on. We don't want to lose his trail in the dark," she commanded.

The twins ran from tree to tree like silent squirrels, following after Fink's elongated shadow. When Fink reached Town Square, the twins hid behind the front-porch posts of the Hobble Gobble diner and watched him climb the marble steps of Town Hall.

The old man took a key from the cuff of his overcoat and opened one of the front doors.

"The Council Of Elders must be meeting tonight," Scooter whispered, noticing the silhouettes of aged Hobblers in the upstairs windows. "But we can't get into Town Hall this late without a key."

Stokely looked up and smiled. "Come on. I think I know another way inside."

The Council Of Elders was in crisis.

Three of its most esteemed members—Happy Gumbledump, Guffy Tinklepot, and Mayor Winky Waddletub—were gone, and the remaining Elders were left uncertain and in disagreement over Hobble's future. Lilla Humplestock stepped up to the podium of the meeting hall and motioned for the white-wigged attendants to take a seat.

"Please calm down," Mayor Humplestock pleaded to the frantic Elders. "We have many issues to discuss tonight, and we haven't the time for fruitless bickering. Our fellow Hobblers will be looking to us for strength, and we must not let them down."

The commotion of the Elders abated, and each took their assigned seats.

The council met at least once a month to discuss the needs and concerns of the town. But with the murders and the Mayor's disappearance, the Elders had called an emergency meeting.

"I beg you, fellow council members, to keep the details of this meeting completely secret. It may be discussed among yourselves, but must never travel beyond this circle," Mayor Humplestock implored. "As you know, three of our Elders—our friends—are no longer with us. Though we do not know Winky's whereabouts, the circumstances of the gatekeepers' murders are very grim. Very grim, indeed. Our beloved friends Happy and Guffy were—" Lilla paused. Tears formed in her grey eyes, and the Elders moved to the edge of their seats. "The truth is—we haven't yet found their bodies."

Many Elders gasped.

Ames Seedbottom stood up at the back of the courtroom, and asked, "If we haven't seen the bodies, then how do we know they're dead?"

Commotion erupted throughout the room.

"We were sent a very clear message," Mayor Humplestock looked across the room at Widow Tinklepot, who wore a black veil and sniffled into a satin handkerchief. "That is all I will say of the matter until more is determined."

C.C. Pottleman, the council's wealthiest member, bellowed, "Murdered comrades! Missing corpses! The mark of the ¥! We must have vengeance!" He pounded his fists so hard on the table in front of him, his white wig fell off.

A few of the Elders cheered.

"Sheriff Hopscotch is undertaking an investigation the likes of which Hobble has never seen," Mayor Humplestock assured. "We *will* get to the bottom of this."

"Sheriff Hopscotch is a buffoon, and we all know it to be true. This is an act of war!" C.C. Pottleman cried out. "The murders took place on the night the Jypsis and Outskirters came into town. What more do we need to know? And don't tell me it's the Vothlor. I was *there* when we destroyed them once and for all. This is the work of them Jypsis. If they want the wrath of Hobble, they shall have it! I vote to resurrect the militia!"

Babby Seedbottom stood up and motioned for Ames, her husband, to stand next to her. "How are Ames and I to gather wild seeds for the orchards if we cannot journey into the forests beyond the town walls? If there's no protection, we'll surely be the next victims!" Babby declared.

Right then, a deep, peaceful voice silenced the tense gathering. It was the voice of an old man, as wise as the rivers and the trees.

"We are weakest when fear rules in our hearts," Pappy Cricklewood declared. "The Vothlor—whether they be working from outside Hobble or from within—have no power over us until we fear them. Fear invites the nightmares, remember? And the nightmares control the heart. To jump to hasty conclusions is both foolish and dangerous. Let us not yet disturb our relations with the Jypsis and Outskirters. Instead, let us go on with our daily duties, and face this darkness with mindful courage, rather than with fear."

Pappy was among the most respected members of the Council. He sat down, and motioned for Lilla Humplestock, whose leadership he had reluctantly approved, to continue her conduction of the meeting.

"Thank you, Nicodemus," Lilla said. "Our first order of business must be the security of Hobble. The gates and watchtowers must be guarded around the clock. We have already instituted a rotation of temporary gatekeepers, as well as watchmen for the towers. But there is still one corner of Hobble left unguarded."

Each of the Elders understood Lilla's meaning, and shuddered at the thought of it.

"Is anyone here willing to stand guard atop the Forbidden Watchtower?" she asked. "It must be manned. We must keep a close watch on the Lostwood from all directions."

A stark heaviness fell upon the room. Not a single hand raised amongst the circle of Elders.

All of a sudden, the most unexpected Elder of all raised his hand high into the air. Everyone's brows raised in surprise at the man who was infamous for his dark history with the Vothlor.

"Fink?" Mayor Humplestock asked in surprise.

The Council slowly turned to look at the retired farmer.

"I'll do it, Mayor," Fink volunteered. "Please, send me. Me and no one else."

From inside the chimney of the courtroom, Scooter and Stokely had heard every word.

33

Chapter 8:

Through The Fog

The next night, Scooter and Stokely were staked out in a cypress tree with a clear view of the Forbidden Watchtower.

Far away in Town Square, they heard the Clock Tower ring twelve times.

Soon after, footsteps thudded through the woods, and Fink emerged from the brambles, panting and out of breath. He carried a lantern in one hand, and dragged a small rowboat with the other. The old man dropped his skiff at the edge of the swamp and looked over both his shoulders, as if expecting to meet someone.

He cleared his throat and shouted out to the watchtower.

"It's me! Fink Karbunkle! I just want you to know I'm here and I mean you ghosts no harm."

From their treetop perch, the Scabbins twins listened with rapt curiosity. An icy chill blew across the haunted swamp, and Fink's top hat blew away. He reached to snatch it, but it sank swiftly into the swampy waters.

The old man cursed, and pushed the small boat off from the muddy shore, rowing right beneath Scooter and Stokely's hideaway.

Scooter gazed across the swamp at the Forbidden Watchtower, and softly nudged Stokely with his elbow.

"Look," Scooter whispered, pointing at the watchtower.

Stokely looked at the roof. The flickering light had returned.

Fink had fastened his lantern to the nose of the boat, and a soft glow reflected upon the green surface of the swamp. He dipped his oars and took a right at the first fork in the waterway, threading farther into the winding channels of the swamp. Frogs croaked from atop the scattered lily pads, and diamond-headed snakes slithered into holes along the bank.

"What do you think he's *really* up to?" Stokely whispered.

"Nothing good," Scooter replied, fixated on the light at the top of the Forbidden Watchtower.

"What—what do you think is out there?" Stokely asked, pretending not to be afraid.

Scooter sat in silence, trying to piece together a connection between Fink and all the recent tragedies in town, but could make no sense of the clues he and Stokely had gathered since the night of the Star Festival.

"Stoke, I just can't figure this out—yet," Scooter finally replied, frustrated by his lack of answers.

"Nothing makes sense," Stokely continued. "Why in the name of Hobble would Fink volunteer to go out to the Forbidden Watchtower *alone*? You think—you think that watchtower is where he killed all those kids? And if he had something to do with Winky's disappearance, he sure isn't acting like it."

Just then, Scooter pointed towards a yellow dot of lanternlight—Fink had made it to the watchtower. The twins watched as Fink climbed up the outdoor stairwell.

When Fink reached the roof of the tower, his lantern hung side by side with another flickering light. After just a moment, he descended the staircase in a violent rush as the other light followed after him. A shrill cry echoed across the swamp.

The breeze stopped blowing, and the frogs stopped croaking.

A long stillness followed.

And then, a deep, sinister laughter rippled across the murky waters.

"What—was—that?" Stokely asked.

Right then, Fink's rowboat burst through the faraway mist like a bird through a cloud. The old man was rowing with all his might back toward the other bank.

Then, a second boat sliced through the fog a few dozen feet behind Fink.

But this second boat had no captain.

The oars were rowed by invisible hands.

"Go away! Leave me be! Leave me be!" Fink cried out, on the verge of tears. "I'm innocent, I swear it! Please, have mercy!"

The second boat was closing in on Fink.

36

The old man had not yet made it to shore when he leapt from his boat and flopped into the grimy waters. He swam desperately and crawled onto the muddy shore, all the while crying out for help. As he turned to view his relentless pursuer, the invisible rower lifted the paddles into the second boat and glided onto the bank.

Fink turned and ran towards the nearby woods, stumbling along as he sought the solace of town.

Once Fink was long gone, the boat reversed its course, and the invisible hands rowed back to the haunted watchtower from whence it had come.

Chapter 9:

Twilight Tellings

Just before dawn, Scooter and Stokely finally found the courage to climb down from their hideout and return to the Pumpkin House. They both hoped to sneak into their beds unnoticed before Gabbo awoke for his work in the fields.

The twins crossed the twilight fields and looked at the enchanted house with a sense of relief and hope. They softly opened the front door to their cinnamon-scented home.

There, sitting in his rocking chair and bathed in candlelight, was their father, whittling a twig with his favorite pocketknife.

"And just what have you two been doing?" Gabbo asked from the shadows.

Scooter and Stokely fumbled for a suitable answer. They had broken the house rules by not being in their bunks by midnight.

"We lost track of time, that's all," Scooter explained.

"Won't happen again, Pa. I promise."

"Very well," Gabbo replied, settled on the matter. "But since you're already awake, you can go milk the cows and gather the eggs for breakfast. Also, draw some water so your brothers and sisters can take a bath. This house is beginning to smell like the creek." He paused, and added, "And go ahead and chop some extra firewood. You can take my axe from the shed. You'll want to finish before lunch, since you have a few pumpkin deliveries to make this afternoon."

Scooter and Stokely sighed and walked back toward the door, silently accepting their punishment.

"Oh, and one more thing," Gabbo called after them.

The twins turned, and Gabbo pointed to an envelope nailed just above the doorway.

"Found it pinned above the door when I woke up. It's addressed to the both of you," he explained. "Don't know why it wasn't sent through the Breezemail."

Stokely cautiously unpinned the mysterious note. The twins exchanged a curious glance, tore open the envelope, and lifted out the letter.

The message was clear and simple:

> *I know what you have seen. You are dealing with something far more ancient and deadly than you can possibly imagine. Meet me on the steps of Town Hall at a quarter 'til midnight tonight.*
> *Trust No One.*
> *-Tripper Boneglaze*

Chapter 10:

Secrets Are Sharper Than Swords

A few candles burned in the windows of nearby shops. Stokely gripped Tripper's letter in her hand as she and Scooter walked up the marble steps of Town Hall.

"I have a bad feeling about all of this," Scooter admitted. "Over a dozen kids have disappeared in the last few days, and here we are, all alone at midnight without a soul to hear us if we scream."

"You're always worryin' too much," Stokely replied. "Besides, Tripper will be here soon."

Right then, the golden cauldron slid backwards, and a small opening appeared. A familiar pair of cocoa-colored eyes peered up at the twins from the darkness below.

"This way," Tripper's voice whispered from the underground passageway. He motioned for Scooter and Stokely to follow him into the dark world beneath the Immortal Flame.

The twins looked at one another in hesitation, then

after dropping half a dozen feet, they landed upon some cobblestones. In the darkness, the twins heard a cranking sound, and looked up to see the cauldron move back into its original position.

Immediately, a torch erupted nearby and illuminated Tripper's face.

"I'm so glad you decided to come," he whispered. "Now, follow me."

Tripper guided the twins down an ancient passageway directly beneath Town Hall.

"I asked you to meet me tonight because there is something you need to know." Tripper paused and slowed his steps, before continuing, "You see, very few twins are born in Hobble."

The three of them arrived at the base of a narrow staircase, which spiraled a hundred yards up into the highest part of a stone tower. Tripper began to climb, and the twins followed in silence.

"There's a special bond which exists between twins. And in that bond, there is unique power and responsibility."

They had climbed the narrow staircase for several stories, but still could see no end in sight.

Tripper continued, "I have sensed this strong power within your bond, and I believe you are both worthy of being invited into an ancient tradition."

"What kind of tradition? Warrior Guards? Lostwood Scouts?" Scooter questioned.

Tripper stepped forward and leaned down toward the twins.

"The Spymasters. We are the most secret sector of the

Armiji," he answered.

"I've read all about the warriors of Light in the Armiji," Scooter proclaimed. "But I've never read anything about any *Spymasters*."

"I s'pose that is because it is a secret well-kept," Tripper replied, grinning from ear to ear. "We Spymasters are an ancient fraternity of Hobblers who bring to light all that hides in darkness. Quite simply, we are the keepers of Hobble's secrets. Without our help, the Old War would have surely been lost to the Vothlor, and Malivar never would have been sent to the void."

Scooter looked at his sister, then back up at Tripper.

"So no one knows about the Spymasters? Not even the Council Of Elders?" Scooter questioned.

"That is correct," Tripper said. "And now that Hobble has entered a new time of grave danger, it will need new spies. You see, sometimes secrets are sharper than swords. If you become one of us, it will be your sacred duty to disarm those secrets which could bring harm to Hobble."

"But what sort of secrets?" Stokely asked.

"The ones all around you. The events at the Crescent Gates. What you witnessed at the swamp. Secrets connected to the Old War." Tripper mounted the final step of the staircase, and instructed, "Don't touch anything you are about to see."

Tripper pushed open a black door and extended the torch, revealing a cold room filled with gears, pulleys, and chimes.

Against the farthest wall was a giant, white circle, with twelve dots spread evenly along the perimeter. A lantern glowed in front of the circle. The twins suddenly realized they were in the top of the Clock Tower.

"By the way, you might want to cover your ears," Tripper announced.

Right then, twelve deafening gongs shook the entire room.

"Midnight," Tripper smiled and pointed to the rotating gears. "First lesson for you both: There is always more beneath the surface than what your eyes may perceive."

Tripper walked to a small window in the Clock Tower, and showed Scooter and Stokely the magnificent view of their beloved town.

"Do you wish to uncover the secrets of Hobble as a Spymaster of the Armiji?" Tripper asked, staring out over the town. "And do you promise to tell me *everything* you discover?"

The twins exchanged a brief, knowing glance and nodded in unison.

"Is this like an apprenticeship?" Stokely asked.

"Something like that," Tripper said. "But this *must* remain a secret for all of time. From now on, there can be no secrets between us." He then reached into his trousers pocket and pulled out two grey stones. "Before I forget, I have a gift for the two of you. These are flint rocks. Both are necessary in order to make a spark, and I want each of you to keep one of them. It will serve as a reminder of your need for one another in the dark times to come. Now, do you have any questions which pertain to the matter at hand?"

"Are there any other Spymasters left in the Armiji besides you?" Scooter asked. He took the two flint rocks and handed one of them to Stokely.

43

Tripper looked down at the ground, and shook his head in sadness.

"Not anymore. I now walk alone. That is why I called you both here tonight. If anything happens to me, and I meet the same fate as my Master, then the tradition of the Spymasters must live on through you. You see, my Master—he is dead."

"I'm—I'm sorry. What happened to him?" Stokely asked, noticing a quiver in Tripper's voice.

"He was a fine man—like a father to me. He was on the verge of uncovering a great secret when he was killed at the front gates of Hobble. My Master was Guffy Tinklepot."

Chapter 11

Defending the Family Honor

A few days later, after working in the fields, Scooter and Stokely visited Pudd's Tavern to spy on Fink, a frequent patron of the roadhouse.

Lively music, played by a band of Light miners, filled the place. The men scratched washboards, beat tin lids, tapped spoons, and stomped their booted feet against the wood-planked floor.

Scooter and Stokely climbed up onto two empty bar stools, and scanned the room for any sign of Fink.

"What can I do for yeh?" Pudd asked from behind the counter, shining a glass with a raggedy towel. He was a burly man with bushy, red sideburns and a mustache to match.

"Make it two cinnamon ciders," Stokely ordered.

"Comin' right up!" Pudd lifted two mugs from behind the counter, flipped a spout attached to a wooden barrel, and filled the glasses. He set the drinks in front of Scooter and Stokely and tossed the towel onto his shoulder. "That'll be half a token for each."

The twins paid for their drinks, took a sip of the foamy cider, and sighed in delight.

"Have you thought any more about what Tripper said last night?" Stokely asked her brother.

"All morning," Scooter answered. "You?"

"I guess so," Stokely answered. "I like my flint-rock."

Just then, Pudd lifted a few recent editions of the *Hobble Gazette* from behind the counter and began tacking them on the wall. The tavern owner had kept a copy of every newspaper since the night of the Star Festival.

"Meteorites, murders, vanished kids, and a missing mayor. What's this town coming to?" Pudd grumbled. He then pinned up the recent article which featured Rinky's pumpkin farmer rankings.

With that, Fink stood up from his table in the shadowed corner of the tavern and chugged the last half of his drink. He was sitting with Tobo Jingles and Nittle Nightbrook. The old man walked up and stood directly behind the twins.

"Take it down, Pudd," Fink demanded, clenching his fists in anger. "How dare you slander my name by posting this rubbish!"

Scooter and Stokely wheeled around on their barstools to see the old man glaring at them.

"Leave it up!" Stokely called out to the bartender and scowled right back at Fink.

Pudd remained with his hands on the newspaper, uncertain as to whether Fink or Stokely was the greater danger.

"I said take it down!" Fink demanded. "These are just a couple of rotten tots."

"And I say you're just a *murderer*! A Vothlor spy, right here in Hobble!" Stokely cried out.

No one had openly called Fink a murderer since the trial declared him innocent nearly fifty years before. The old man's eyes twitched with rage.

"Why, you little . . . You don't know anything! You can't even begin to understand the real truth. But here's what I do know. Gabbo Scabbins is the worst farmer in the history of Hobble! And I bet it's *him* stealing all those kids, and keepin' 'em beneath the Pumpkin House. I bet it's him who's working for the Voth—"

Before Fink finished his last word, Stokely had slugged him in the stomach with her left fist and Scooter had jumped onto his back.

The band struck up a new tune which matched the rhythm of the fight. As the twins pulled at Fink's ears and hair, he spun in circles, trying to fling them off his shoulders.

"Get off, you stinkin' leeches!" he cried. "Lemme go!"

Scooter wrapped his arms around Fink's neck and squeezed with all his might, turning the old man's face redder than a tomato. Stokely picked up her mug and tossed the remaining cider into his eyes.

Fink groaned and spun his way across the room, knocking over tables, spilling drinks, and forcing the excited onlookers to dive out of the way.

Suddenly, the crowd grew silent.

Sherriff Hopscotch and Deputy Notwod had run into

the tavern and were yanking the twins off Fink. Scooter and Stokely tried to kick themselves free, but Sherriff whipped out his handcuffs and locked their hands behind their backs. Fink dashed out into the alleyway behind the tavern.

"What's the meaning of all this?" Sheriff demanded. "You two have been a public disturbance one too many times! Tearing up a fine establishment like Pudd's Tavern! And during this time when honest folks are already in a fright. The last thing we need is a couple of wild goblins makin' a ruckus."

"But—!" Scooter cried out.

"Tut-tut," Deputy Notwod interrupted. "Don't be making excuses, now."

The lawmen led the twins outside and towards the jailhouse.

As soon as they left, Pudd rose up from behind the bar with a wearied look on his face. The bar fight had been the third one that month. Everyone's skeleton seemed to be in a twist over the recent happenings. He took a broom and walked around the bar to sweep up the mess of scattered playing cards, broken glass, and peanut shells.

Just as Pudd swept the last of the mess into a dustpan, Kel Clovestar—the writer, director, and producer of Hobble's silent films—stepped through the swinging doors and tapped his cane against the sawdust floor.

"Did you hear the news, Pudd?" Kel asked.

"What news?" Pudd replied, dumping shattered glass and peanut shells into a nearby trashcan.

"Three more kids gone missing last night! Last anyone heard, the trio had ventured toward the swamp."

Chapter 12:

Everyone Must Choose A Side

Sherriff Hopscotch sorted through the giant ring hanging from his belt, and finally found the key to unlock the prison cell of the Hobble Jailhouse. The shadowy room was empty except for a single bunk bed, two wooden stools, and a barred window. Sheriff opened the door and shoved the handcuffed twins into the lonesome chamber.

"I run the show here," Sheriff declared, slightly out of breath. "I say what you can and cannot do. There's to be no roughhousing. No complaining. No game-making. No gambling. No—"

Sinister laughter interrupted Sheriff's soliloquy.

The twins turned around, and saw a lanky, ratty-haired prisoner crouched at the back of the cell. The stranger's laughter filled the quiet jailhouse, and Sheriff's face turned red with fury.

"Something funny, Wigglesworth?" Sheriff demanded.

The prisoner stood to his bare feet and walked into the

dusty sunbeam pouring through the barred window. A crooked scar jutted over his left eye.

"Something's funny alright, Sheriff," Crook Wigglesworth replied, grabbing onto the iron bars with his right hand.

"Well, what's the joke?" Sheriff demanded.

"*You're* the joke, Hopscotch," Crook replied in a sinister voice. "You think by arresting children and stuffing your face with cupcakes you can save Hobble. But a time is coming when you'll be revealed for what you truly are. A dark time is coming indeed. I happen to know for a fact that the Vothlor are still alive. One of 'em has been hiding here among you in Hobble for fifty years—right beneath your noses. Waiting for the Black Candle to be lit, when Malivar will return and empower his secret vessel. And on that day, I'll walk out of here with your blood on the bottom of my boots."

So the Black Candle does exist, Scooter thought. *Did Tripper lie to us?*

Sheriff was silent a moment. "Ah, shutup! Don't listen to him, kids. He's crazy as a loon. Destined for the gallows, he is. Three months and five days, ain't it Wigglesworth?" he asked.

Sheriff turned and sat down at his desk, where he had indeed hidden a box of blueberry cupcakes beneath his chair.

Crook sat back down on the floor of the cell.

"Wha—what's the Black Candle?" Stokely asked.

Without raising his head, Crook answered, "You'll know soon enough. Just make sure you're on the right side when the time comes. Everyone must choose a side. When

—
50

the nightmares start coming to you, then you'll know which side to choose."

"We'll choose the Armiji," Scooter assured.

"Fools," Crook scoffed. "Fighting for what? A town filled with secrets and traitors? Your warriors are old and your mayor is dead. Ain't no one can help this town—especially not a bunch of measly rugrats like yourself."

The words pierced through the twins.

"Winky may not be dead," Stokely corrected with a faltering voice. "He's just—just gone."

Crook nodded his head. "He's dead, alright. I happen to know it for a fact."

The twins sat themselves on the wooden bench and looked over at Sheriff, who sat with his boots propped up on the desk, sneaking bites of blueberry cupcakes. After a few minutes, he nodded off to sleep.

As soon as Sheriff's eyes closed, a folded, white piece of paper tied to a fishing line was lowered through a crack in the ceiling above the twins' heads. Stokely was the first to notice the dangling message. She nudged Scooter, and placed a finger over her mouth.

They both looked toward Sheriff, snoring like a porch dog.

The piece of paper landed in Scooter's lap. He unfolded the note, and he and Stokely read the familiar handwriting.

> *Scooter and Stokely,*
> *In fifteen seconds, Sheriff will receive a letter in his breezebox. I am confident that after he reads it, you will be released.*
> *At sunset tomorrow, walk northeast on*

the Light Train rails. Look for the 'X' and
I'll be near. Bring your camping packs.
We're taking a trip into the Lostwood.

Behold The Power Of Secrets!
-Tripper

A moment later, the breezebox whirred in the corner, awakening Sheriff, who rose from his chair and snatched the newly arrived letter. He read the message, then held the letter above a candle's flame until it caught fire. He then tossed it into the empty hearth and watched it burn.

Once the letter had curled into black crisps, Sheriff frantically searched through his ring of keys.

"It seems I made a terrible mistake earlier this afternoon," Sheriff said. "No crime committed today. None at all. Just a slight misunderstanding."

Sheriff unlocked the prison cell and opened the barred door.

"Come on out of there, kids. You're free to go," he said. "Make sure your friend knows that I did you no harm. And send him my best regards."

Just before the twins exited the jailhouse, Crook called out, "Remember kids, you don't have to defend a town filled with traitors and secrets. Everyone you think you can trust is already working for the Vothlor. You might as well receive the mark, and save yourselves from the massacre to come."

Chapter 13:

The Tree Of Memories

"Follow me, and try to keep up," Tripper said as soon as the twins arrived the next day at the meeting location. "The faster you walk, the less likely your scent will be traced by goblins."

"But how did you convince Sheriff to let us go?" Scooter asked.

"Everyone has secrets, lad," Tripper explained. "And most Hobblers want to keep 'em that way."

Without another word, Tripper turned and headed off into a maze of the Lostwood's giant, whispering timbers. The twins exchanged a nervous glance, then scurried after him, ducking beneath twisting limbs, clambering over fallen logs, and charging through thorny thickets, as they tried to match his pace.

When Tripper stopped at the edge of a foggy glen, he

turned and said, "We're here. From this moment on, you must remain as quiet as a hoodwink."

Scooter and Stokely followed Tripper into a narrow pathway of dead, knee-high grass. A puffy, white fog completely shrouded the path, and the air smelled of fresh honeysuckle and vanilla.

Then they saw it.

An enormous tree rose up from the leaf-covered ground, dwarfing every surrounding tree and shrub. Its gnarled trunk was a dozen times as wide as the Pumpkin House. Its limbs and branches grew higher into the darkening sky than the twins were able to see.

"Wh—What is this?" Scooter whispered in bewilderment.

"This tree is the last of its kind. You may call it the Tree Of Memories, as the Ancients called it," Tripper responded. "It speaks the collective wisdoms of fallen Armiji warriors, and knows all things they once knew. Consider it a library of forgotten secrets."

When the twins looked closer at the tree, they saw what appeared to be an ancient face formed into the bark. The face looked wise and strong, yet gentle.

Tripper continued in a whisper, "All Spymasters come here at the beginning of their journey. The Tree Of Memories will reveal to you a glimpse of your destiny, but you must quiet your hearts in order to hear its voice. Step forward, and listen."

Scooter and Stokely obeyed in reverent silence, listening closely for any revelation. But the once soft wind blew harder and harder with each step Scooter and Stokely took towards the tree. A pinwheel of strange images flashed before their disbelieving eyes: Fink Karbunkle, the Forbidden Watchtower, the misty form near the swamp, the empty rowboat, the mark of the 𝖞 imprinted in the mud.

A wise, ancient voice floated through the white fog: "The two of you are strongest when together, and weakest when apart. You must never separate. Only by this bond shall you survive the dark time to come. A time will come, when you must die for one another."

Suddenly, a wild wind ripped through the branches of the Tree Of Memories, and a tornado of leaves and fog blew between Scooter and Stokely, preventing them from seeing or hearing one another. They stumbled in the supernatural storm, and called out for one another.

A wicked voice whispered into their thoughts, "*Give me your souls and you will survive the time to come. Do not trust in the Armiji. They lie to you. The man who stands beside you now, stands with me.*"

Stokely screamed out and covered her ears, and Scooter ran to her side.

Then, a horrific vision entered into Scooter's mind. He saw the walls of the Pumpkin House bashed down into a pulp. He burst through the frame where the front door had once been, and saw every member of his family lying on the ground, dead. The bloody mark of the 𝖞 was carved into their foreheads. Scooter rushed to the place where Stokely lay, sucking in her final breaths.

"Stokely!" he called, shaking his sister. "Stokely, please! Don't die! Stokely!"

The next thing Scooter knew, Tripper had tackled him

to the ground. He shook the boy with all his might, and Scooter escaped the nightmarish vision.

The voice of darkness trailed away into the Lostwood. The wind died down, and the fog cleared. Scooter and Stokely looked at one another in horror.

"The nightmares," Tripper whispered. "It—it was him, wasn't it? It was Malivar. You must never tell anyone what you heard tonight. As soon as you spread the fear, his power will grow."

But Scooter could not help it.

He felt fear rising up inside of him like a mountain of fire, and he knew he had to tell someone—anyone.

Chapter 14:

Tales And Tellings

The campfire blazed as Tripper and the Scabbins twins roasted marshmallows to a perfect, golden crust.

"Who wants to hear a ghost story?" Tripper proposed, his face taking on the orange glow of the firelight.

He had been trying to lighten the mood all night, but the twins were in no mood for gamemaking. The schoolteacher took a bite of his golden marshmallow and playfully growled as the melted treat dripped from the corners of his lips.

Scooter looked up at the Tree Of Memories, which was filled with the tiny flickers of a thousand fireflies.

"Maybe another night," Scooter said, pulling the brim of his straw hat low over his eyes and leaning back against a fallen log.

"Then how about an ancient Hobble riddle?" Tripper said.

"Fine," Scooter groggily replied. " Go on with it."

Stokely groaned. She hated riddles.

"Listen closely. You never know when such knowledge could save your life," Tripper said. "Here it is: *I am greater than the Light and more evil than the Darkness. The poorest Hobblers have me, the richest Hobblers need me. And if you eat me, you will die. What am I?*"

"Poison," Scooter immediately answered.

"Try again," Tripper said.

Scooter leaned back, and sighed. "I'll have it figured out by the morning. Just you wait. Say, Tripper, are you sure it's safe to sleep out here? What if—I guess I'm just worried Malivar may know we're out here."

"Don't worry about Malivar," Tripper answered. "At least, not tonight."

Stokely sat up.

"Tripper, there's something I've been wondering about," she said.

"And what might that be?" Tripper asked.

"The Black Candle. We know it exists, and that you aren't telling us everything you know about it."

Scooter immediately sat up.

A shadow crept over Tripper's face, and his eyes grew wide as two moons.

"Who told you such a thing?" he asked, solemnly.

"We heard Winky tell Fink you were the one who reported it missing," Scooter replied. "And we heard Crook Wigglesworth say that whenever it's lit, Malivar's comin' back. What did he mean by that?"

Tripper looked over both his shoulders, and leaned in closer to the fire. His eyes darted back and forth between

Scooter and Stokely.

"You must never tell anyone what I'm about to tell you," Tripper said. "If you desire to be a possessor of secrets, then you must learn how to keep them."

"We promise," Stokely quickly assured.

Scooter nodded in agreement.

"On the morning you came to visit me at the creek, I did not feel it was the right time to reveal anything about the Black Candle. Very few Hobblers know of its existence, and even a very few is too many. I told you that my teacher, Guffy Tinklepot, was on the verge of uncovering one of the greatest secrets ever to exist within the walls of Hobble— and perhaps even in the Lostwood beyond. Alas, he died before his work was finished."

"What's that have to do with the Black Candle?" Stokely asked.

Tripper leaned forward, and the firelight blazed in his eyes.

"He was about to find out how to destroy the Black Candle once and for all. Not just seal it away, but actually *destroy* it. There would be no chance of Malivar's resurrection if it was destroyed, and the Vothlor would never have power again," Tripper whispered.

Scooter and Stokely looked at one another in confusion.

"What's so dangerous about a stupid candle? Can't they just melt it down or sink it in the creek or something?" Stokely asked.

"If only it were that easy. This candle is made of the very fabric of souls—dark souls—from long, long ago," Tripper explained with a grimace. "It has the power to plant evil seeds in even the most noble of hearts. Malivar speaks through it, just as he speaks in nightmares. At the end of the Old War, the Black Candle was captured and sealed away in a secret crypt. Other treasures of immense power, beauty, and wickedness were buried in the crypt as well—a Time Crystal to influence the past and the future, and a magical map which allowed its keeper to know the locations of everything in existence, from Hobblers to beasts to doorways. And, of course, there were other relics as well. Most of those relics have since been removed, but the Black Candle remained sealed away. Only those who buried it were supposed to know its secret location. And for fifty years, Malivar and his nightmares have been silenced. But a few hours before Guffy was killed, he told me the Black Candle had been stolen. That is why the nightmares are slowly beginning to seep back into Hobble. I fear they will only get stronger."

A hollow wind rustled through the tree above, and a rainfall of leaves fell upon the cackling fire. Scooter and Stokely sat in awed silence.

"Now, it's time for you two to go to bed," Tripper said. "Once you are officially initiated into the Spymasters, I will tell you more."

But before Tripper turned to lay out his sleeping pad, Stokely shot a glance at Scooter.

She cleared her throat and began, "So what's gonna happen? Once the candle's lit, is Malivar going to attack Hobble?"

Tripper lifted a stick out of the fire and stoked the flames. He took a deep breath, and sighed. "Chances are, Malivar has always been in Hobble, hibernating within one or two vessels who remained covert after the Old War. He's probably just waiting for his moment to be resurrected through the Black Candle. You see, Malivar uses others to carry out his will. He is the source of power, but his vessels are the ones who commit his dark deeds. His own hands have never touched blood, but he is behind the murders of countless thousands."

"Who could the undercover vessel be?" Scooter asked, remembering that Crook had warned them about the same thing.

Tripper shrugged. "Probably someone with deep ties to the Vothlor from the Old War. That's my guess. But I'm only speculating. Could be anyone, for all we know."

Fink, Scooter thought.

"If Malivar is sealed away inside some Hobbler's soul, then why don't we just get rid of the Hobbler?" Stokely asked.

"If we knew who it was, perhaps that would be the wisest path. Alas, this is one secret we Spymasters have never been able to uncover in all these fifty years," Tripper explained.

"But I thought Spymasters know *everything* that goes on in Hobble," Scooter challenged.

"There are some secrets which even we have yet to unlock. Perhaps you two will help reveal such things."

Chapter 15:

Fink And The Director

The next morning, Stokely picked the lock of the back door of Fink's retirement cottage. They had seen Fink in Town Square a few minutes before, and knew he would not be back home for a while.

Stokely admired the numerous awards, plaques, and trophies which were displayed throughout Fink's trophy room. It seemed that Fink truly had been a great pumpkin farmer.

"You could help me, since this was *your* idea," Scooter said from across the room. He sat at Fink's writing desk and shook a small drawer until it slid open. He searched among a stack of old, crinkled papers for any interesting evidence to link Fink to the Vothlor. After what they had heard last night with Tripper, Scooter and Stokely believed Fink could be the secret vessel hiding Malivar.

As Stokely walked towards Scooter, she noticed a strange, black chest serving as a lamp stand in the corner. She quickly removed the lamp and saw the phrase, 'Ministry Memories' carved into the lid of the chest.

"Scooter! Come look at this!" she called out.

Scooter ran to his sister's side.

Stokely removed the pocketknife from her overalls pocket. She jiggled the blade in the crook of the rusted lock, and opened the chest.

"We might as well take a look, since it's already open," she said, innocently.

The space within was filled with several old pamphlets, handwritten notes, black playing cards, and a few photographs. Scooter quickly filtered through the photos, showing Fink as a young man with a sparkle in his eye.

In most of the photos, Fink stood beside a man in a black robe who wore a dusty top hat. They looked like close friends.

"Who's this guy?" Stokely asked. "He's in just about every picture. Must be seven feet tall."

Right then, a deep, angry voice called out from behind them, "I thought I smelled a couple of rats!"

Scooter dropped the stack of photos into the chest, where they thudded against the cracked wood like a heartbeat.

Fink was standing in the doorway, holding a hatchet.

Chapter 16:

The Fireside Terror

Fink thundered into the room and dumped a few newly-split logs into his fireplace.

"What business have you here?" the old man demanded. "I oughta have you filthy prowlers thrown back in jail for snooping!"

"We—we were hoping to—" Stokely fumbled over her words. "We thought—we thought you might still be working for the Vothlor."

Fink shook his hatchet at the twins and ranted, "For fifty years I've tried to shed that reputation, and for fifty years not a soul has let me forget my regrets! 'Traitor' they say! 'Murderer' they call me! Even the Elders still suspect me of being a spy—I can see it in their eyes. Some even think it was *me* who killed all those children so long ago. But it was Malivar who done it *through* me. I *never* should've received the mark."

Fink touched the back of his neck, where a strange scar glimmered in the sunlight seeping in through the windows.

"But where's the mark now? I thought once a person joins the Vothlor, they're always a Vothlor," Scooter said.

"That's what Malivar would like you to think. But there are ways to change back from the dark path."

"How—how did you change?"

"I took the mark because I felt there wasn't much else to live for. Malivar did terrible things through me—unspeakable things—but all the while a sliver of Light remained alive inside me. It was that tiny sliver that turned me back from my wicked ways. Malivar had already killed all the children by possessing my body and murdering them with my hatchet. If they didn't take the mark, he ended their lives. Courageous, those little ones. Standing before the Darkness itself and remaining faithful to the Light to the end. I think of them every day—their faces give me strength. They didn't die in vain, you know. If ever there was a reason to hope in the Light, it was them."

"But how did you shed the mark?" Scooter questioned.

"It was a special knife that cut it from my neck. Nicodemus Cricklewood—who you probably know as Pappy—used a black blade to free me from the mark. He and Winky both testified at my trial. I owe them both my life for what they did, standing up for me in that way."

Fink walked to an armchair near the fireplace and collapsed with a melancholy sigh. He poked the embers of the fire with the hatchet until they caught flame. The orange light cast shadows upon his wrinkled face, and he lightly tapped his black ruby ring on the handcrafted arm of the chair.

"Now, put those things away and come join an old man by the fire," he said warmly, to the twins' bewildered surprise.

Stokely obediently closed the chest and placed the lamp back on top of it. The twins walked to the fireplace and sat upon the ground at Fink's feet.

"We—we're just curious about everything going on, that's all," Scooter explained.

Fink sighed and said, "I must admit, I was in quite a fright when I saw the back door cracked open. I thought—well—I thought the dark vapor had come to kill me for what I had seen at the Forbidden Watchtower."

"What do you mean—'dark vapor'?" Stokely asked.

Fink poked the fire again and slipped off his boots.

"As citizens of Hobble, you have a right to know the truth, even if your Pa *is* Gabbo Scabbins." Fink paused, then whispered, "Children, I've been visited again by Malivar."

The gnarled logs popped in the fireplace as Scooter and Stokely listened in excitement and suspicion.

Fink leaned towards the twins and began his tale. "You see, Mayor Humplestock recently asked the Elders for a volunteer to guard the Forbidden Watchtower. Being the former head pumpkin farmer, and a darned good one at that, I knew I was more familiar with the northeastern corner of Hobble than anyone else. So the next night, I took a rowboat and a lantern across the swamp and tied my vessel at the watchtower's dock. I moseyed around and gazed up at the tower. A light burned on the roof, and I took the outer staircase to see what it was. As I began to climb up, that's when I felt it."

"Felt what?" Stokely asked.

Fink was silent for a moment. "The presence of *him*—Malivar. Hadn't felt it in fifty years, but it was him alright, sure as night," he replied, nervously. "I climbed, and I climbed, by the light of my lantern, ignoring the haunts of the watchtower. And then, at the top of the stairs, I could see the faint glow of a second light! I thought it a bright star at the time, but soon realized it was another lantern—floating in mid-air."

"What was it?" Scooter asked.

Fink poked the fire once more, and his voice lowered to a quivering whisper. "I stepped onto the roof and called out to whatever it was. Right when I spoke, the lantern began to move . . . but no hand held it! It just floated there, as if by Jypsi magic. I thought my eyes were playing tricks on me. But the lantern moved closer, and suddenly I was chilled through my bones! I could scarcely take a breath! And then, bless me soul, I saw a vision I shall never forget. I saw Mayor Waddletub, clear as day. I ran to embrace him, but the vision disappeared like ashes carried away by the wind. And then I saw Red Crisp, Hoot Cricklewood, and all the other kids who've gone missing this October. All of 'em crying in the darkness. Screaming. Lost. But they, too, disappeared, and turned into a pile of skulls. All vanished but the lantern."

"The nightmares," Stokely mused, her face paled by Fink's revelation.

Fink continued, "After the vision faded, I ran like any other Hobbler would have done. And now, every time I close my eyes, I imagine the poor faces of those children.

Some nights I awake from nightmares only to see the lantern floating outside my bedroom window. I've a mind to purchase some curtains!"

Fink stood from his armchair and looked down at the twins, who sat speechless. "Promise me you won't set foot near the swamp, especially with Hallows Eve being so near. That's the only night when Malivar can be conjured," Fink demanded. "I wouldn't curse anyone with the things I've seen!"

"I promise," Stokely replied.

"Me too," Scooter said.

"Good," Fink paused and looked down at Scooter. The old man leaned forward and whispered a chilling warning, "Because I saw your face too, boy—alongside them missing kids."

Chapter 17:

A Parting Gift

Nittle Nightbrook had been the librarian in Hobble ever since she was given the apprenticeship as a young girl. She was now an old woman, who wore long black dresses and always had her pointed nose buried deep in a tome. The library sat next to the Museum Of Wonders, and Nittle knew the location of every book, and could point Hobblers to the exact page and passage of their desire. Alas, she worked from sunrise to sundown seven days a week, and rarely left the premises.

Scooter and Stokely opened the heavy library doors and walked up to the information desk, where Nittle was organizing books onto a cart.

"Late fees are one token for every day the book has been overdue," Nittle declared without looking up from her work.

"We don't have any overdue books," Stokely said. "We were just wantin' to check out one."

"Which book?"

"Any book, really—as long as it's about the Vothlor, and the mark of the ⚡."

Nittle immediately stopped her work, and looked up at the twins.

"The mark of the ⚡?" Nittle asked.

"Yeah, and we need to know where Malivar's been all this time."

Nittle shuffled toward the twins and bent down. They could smell her stale breath breathing into their faces.

"Sorry, there are no books on those subjects."

"Nothing? But they're—"

Before Scooter could finish, Nittle hissed and dug her sharp fingernails into his shoulder. She jerked him close and warned, "I said no books, boy! I know this library like the back of my hand, and I said *no books!*"

Scooter wrenched himself free and stumbled backwards. Stokely ran over to check on her brother.

Nittle stood with hands on her hips, her head cocked to one side.

"I think we'll just go," Stokely said. "Come on, Scoot."

As they turned to leave the vast sanctuary of books, Nittle called after them, "Oh, darling. I think I have something of yours."

Stokely turned around, just as Nittle tossed a marble towards her. Stokely caught it, and glared up at the librarian.

"Th—thanks," Stokely said, immediately recognizing it as one of the marbles she had left at the swamp. "Come on, Scoot. We need to leave Miss Nightbrook to her work."

Chapter 18:

In The Skeleton's Hand

Several nights later, Scooter and Stokely rowed across the swamp in a boat they had borrowed indefinitely from C.C. Pottleman, although Pottleman was not actually aware he had lent them the boat.

"Death," Scooter mused aloud. "No, that can't be it."

"What are you talkin' about?"

Scooter glanced up. "Oh, sorry. I'm still workin' through the riddle Tripper asked in the Lostwood. I can't figure it out for the life of me."

Stokely rolled her eyes at the mention of such trivia, and continued rowing.

"There's way more important things to talk about than some silly little riddle."

"You're right. But Fink's story was pretty convincing."

"Maybe he really *was* innocent," Stokely said. "Nittle

Nightbrook, on the other hand, seems to know something she's not tellin'. Maybe she's even workin' for Malivar. How else would she have had one of my marbles?"

When the twins arrived at the base of the tower, Scooter glanced up to see if the invisible rower's lantern was flickering atop the roof.

The roof was dark.

"Don't worry. We'll be alright. Just gotta stick together," Stokely assured, noticing her brother's unease.

They tied the boat to the dock and climbed out.

There was a sign at the edge of the dock. It read: *Entrance into the Northeastern Tower is forbidden, decreed by the Council Of Elders.*

Stokely slapped the sign as she strode past.

"This sign ain't meant for us," she said, motioning for Scooter to follow. "Come on, let's get inside. Then maybe we can find some clues about what's really goin' on."

The twins walked to the base of the tower and gazed up at the hundred empty windows staring back at them from the black stone walls. A deep moan bellowed from the dark recesses of the tower, and the soft hum of a funereal song carried on the wind. They circled around to the backside of the tower, and found a narrow entrance overrun with vines. After they cut through the overgrowth with their pocketknives, they entered into an interior staircase.

They ascended through six different landings before they arrived at the top floor, where Stokely found an old torch fastened to the wall.

"Got your half of the flint rock?" she asked.

"Yep."

Stokely struck the two pieces of flint together next to

the head of the torch until it caught a flame. The fiery blaze revealed a network of hallways. One hallway was guarded by a stone warrior holding an outstretched sword.

"I'm guessin' this is the right one," Stokely whispered, flipping open her pocketknife.

Scooter and Stokely crept past the sculpture and into a dark chamber, but came to a sudden stop.

There, slumped next to a massive door, was a yellow-boned skeleton. It wore a collared, black shirt with leather straps crisscrossed over its shoulders. A tiny, white diamond glimmered at the center of the cross belt, just over the place where the skeleton's heart had once been. A satchel lay next to the skeleton.

"I don't see the mark of the ⚡ anywhere," Scooter said, examining the skeleton's garments.

"What's in the bag?" Stokely asked.

She opened the satchel and peered inside at three iron canisters. Stokely lifted one of the canisters from the satchel and unscrewed the lid. Inside was a weathered scroll. She and Scooter stared at the strange lines and markings on the page, but could not make sense of its meaning.

"It looks like some kind of a map," Stokely finally said.

"But of what? It's not Hobble or the Lostwood," Scooter said as he took the document out of Stokely's hands.

"Maybe it's a map of this watchtower?" Stokely guessed.

Right then, footsteps sounded in the stairwell. Chills scurried up the twins' spines as they wondered upon who, or what, might be approaching.

"Go! Hide!" Scooter whispered to his sister.

He stuffed the map back inside the iron canister, and the twins hid behind a stone pillar. What they saw next changed everything they believed about Hobble.

Chapter 19:

A New Wager

A hooded figure holding a torch walked past Scooter and Stokely's hiding place. After a moment, the twins quietly followed.

Finally, the stranger stopped at a shadowy cavern carved out of the wall. It was blocked off by a dozen rusted bars, and a bright, white lock dangled from the cell's door. Scooter and Stokely muffled their breaths, and listened to the conversation which followed:

A deep, seductive voice spoke from within the shadows of the cell, "Hellooo, old friend."

"How did you know it was me?" the hooded man replied.

"I have been locked away in this cell for fifty years, with only the haunts of the tower to keep me company. But all the while, I've known you would one day return. You've aged, Nicodemus," the unseen prisoner said.

Pappy Cricklewood removed his hood and stared into

75

the darkness of the cell. The prisoner slowly moved forward into the light, and Pappy stared at the man he had known long ago, puzzling at his unchanged appearance. The prisoner wore a dusty black top hat and a black suit; a deck of black cards fluttered between his hands.

"You haven't aged a day," Pappy replied in astonishment.

"It's one of the powers Malivar promised me," the prisoner explained.

Pappy took a step forward.

"I've—I've come to change my wager. I made a mistake," Pappy said.

The prisoner chuckled. "You cannot change such things."

Pappy gripped the cell bars.

"But there must be a way. I thought I was making the right decision, but—but now there is a name and a face to the boy. Now I know his mind, his heart, his potential. I can't take his future away from him."

Scooter and Stokely looked at one another in puzzlement.

Could he be talking about Notch?

The cards continued to dance between the prisoner's hands as he replied, "Remember what you said on the final hour of the Old War, at the cave just before the Black Candle was extinguished and you locked me in this tower? 'Let the boy die young,' you said. 'It is better to sacrifice one than to bring Darkness to the many'."

"But I didn't know what I was doing," Pappy pleaded. "I was young and foolish. Please, let me change it."

"All this while, Hobble has believed you a hero, a

willing martyr. The slayer of countless Vothlor. And yet, all these years, you've allowed *me* to stay alive. You were afraid to kill me because you feared to destroy the keeper of your destiny, but you should have destroyed me when you had the chance. You're not a hero at all, Nicodemus. You're a coward."

The twins could hardly believe what they were hearing. Everyone in Hobble knew Pappy Cricklewood to be one of the greatest heroes of the Old War. No one had ever questioned Pappy's valor. But every word the prisoner spoke made Scooter and Stokely suspect that Cricklewood was not entirely who they had always believed him to be.

"I may be a coward for letting you live," Pappy admitted. "But I've made my decision. If you don't allow me to change my wager, I *will* kill you, come what may of my destiny."

"But you're an old man now. You haven't much destiny left—a few measly years at most. Your gesture is hardly a sacrifice," Silas said.

"That may be. But I will put an end to you if you do not let me change it," Pappy replied.

Silas' voice turned violent, "Fool! If you destroy me, you destroy yourself, for we have been tied together through the bond of your wager. And your grandson is sewn into it as well, as are the destiny of all things."

Pappy stared at the ground.

"There must be another way. I'll do anything."

"*Anything?*" the prisoner questioned.

Pappy nodded.

There was silence for a moment. Ghostly whispers echoed through the chamber.

"There is one way," Silas said, smiling at the haunts to which he had grown accustomed. "But it requires something worth more than the boy's *life*."

"What then?"

Silas removed his top hat, and pressed his face between two bars.

"Your *soul*," he whispered. "Give Malivar your soul, and I will allow you to change your wager, and save your grandson's life. Receive the mark."

"Never," Pappy resounded. "Of all the souls in your keeping, mine will never be among them."

"But you're an old man, with one foot already in the grave. Join him, and he can give you more days, weeks, months, years, even centuries. Besides, you, more than anyone, should know the Light is faltering. Even Waddletub is now dead. The Vothlor is much greater than I am. I am merely a vessel. I have heard whispers that the Black Candle will soon be lit again. Malivar will return, and we who belong to the Vothlor will possess everything you Hobblers have tried to protect: the Black Candle, the Time Crystal, the Omni-map and all that has prevented us from destroying your kind in the past. It is only a matter of time before I am freed from these bars, and I will pick the souls of Hobblers like fruit from a tree. You might as well give me yours now, willingly, that you might *enjoy* the pleasures of the Vothlor, rather than be devoured by them."

Pappy shook his head, and looked down at the ground in anguish.

"What if—what if I let you go free? Will you let me change my wager then?" the old man offered.

"Why would I need you to let me go free? As I said, it is

only a matter of time before Malivar reveals to the Vothlor where I am and how to break the white lock."

"But it may be days, weeks, months. Consider this a truce of sorts. You let me change my wager from the end of the Old War, and a new war begins at the moment of your release."

"Oh, but the new war has already begun. Malivar's whispers have visited me numerous times in recent days to tell me so," Silas assured in a deep, chilling voice. "But since you and I are old acquaintances, I suppose we can play a game. If we win this new war, your grandson will still die young, *and* I shall collect your soul. If we lose, then I will leave the boy's life alone to choose his own fate, and your soul will be left undisturbed. So tell me, Nicodemus, do you believe so strongly in the power of the Light as to rest everything upon it?"

"Before you crossed over to the Vothlor, Silas, you taught us to trust in the Light with all our heart and mind. Some of us still believe in that sentiment, myself included. Did you even believe what you were saying back then? Or were you the Director of the Ministry simply to wield power? Once Malivar came along and promised *more* power to you, you didn't hesitate a moment," Pappy mused aloud.

"Every man has his price," Silas said. "Mine was immortality. To live without aging is greater than all rewards of the Light. Now, what is it you want?"

"I want my grandson to be able to live his life, and choose his own destiny. At all risks. I want him to fight his own war."

Pappy was silent for a moment, then offered his hand through the opening of the bars. Silas shook it, sealing the new deal.

Pappy lifted a key out of his pocket—a key he had considered destroying for the five decades since he first laid eyes upon it—and turned it in the white lock.

Silas stepped out of his cell, free for the first time in fifty years. The prisoner and Pappy stood face to face, with no barriers between them.

"You will never fool Hobble. We didn't allow it during the Old War, and we won't allow it in the war to come."

Silas laughed, "Oh, the Vothlor will be revived soon enough. However, I'm not the one you need to fear at this time. Malivar has found a way to live on these past fifty years. Within the walls of Hobble, in fact. Within one of your own—a Hobbler."

"Impossible. All of the vessels were destroyed."

"I wasn't destroyed. What makes you think there weren't others that somehow escaped as well?"

Silas smiled, then vanished into the shadows.

As Pappy began walking back down the hallway, he stopped and waved his torch into the darkness, sensing someone else's presence.

"Who's there?" the old man called.

Scooter and Stokely fled their hiding place, ran towards a small window, and peered down at the swamp. A hundred feet below, the waters shimmered green in the moonlight.

Stokely turned and whispered, "It's our only escape. Hurry, and grab the other two maps from the skeleton!"

"We don't have time! Jump! Now!" Scooter said in fright, pushing Stokely toward the window before Pappy could catch a glimpse of their faces.

"Hey!" Pappy called, moving towards them. "Show

---

yourself!"

Stokely quickly crawled through the opening and jumped, falling toward the slimy muck below.

As Scooter moved back across the room to grab the other two maps in the skeleton's hand, he heard two heavy boots plodding towards him. Abandoning his pursuit, he darted back to the window and leapt toward the swamp below.

Chapter 20:

The Meaning Of The Map

A week later, the Scabbins twins still had not deciphered the skeleton's map or made sense of the conversation between Pappy and the prisoner named Silas. The clues had become even more complicated since the announcement of Pappy Cricklewood's gruesome murder. They knew everything was connected, but did not know how, or what they could do about it. They sent a letter to Sheriff's office offering to help with the investigation, but a one-line reply came back: *Everyone knows Malivar is dead as a doornail. Stop wasting our time and stirring up fears in town. You've given us enough trouble for one October.*

The next day, an anonymous letter was mailed to the twins, warning them to mind their own business—or else.

After that, the twins decided to keep their investigation to themselves.

"Keep a lookout, Scoot," Stokely instructed as she knelt on the dirt ground.

Scooter latched the outhouse door and looked through the cutout crescent moon toward the Pumpkin House. Smoke poured out of the crooked chimney and faded into the twilight sky. In the distance, Scooter could hear Gabbo's wagon creaking across the lush farmland.

"We're all clear," Scooter announced. "Pa's on his way in from the fields, but he's still half a mile from the house."

Stokely wiped the dirt floor with her hands until she found a red string. She yanked the string, and a box top swung upwards, revealing pocketknives, fireworks, smoke bombs, matches, a few tokens, and other keepsakes the twins kept hidden from the rest of their siblings. Stokely pushed the items aside and lifted out the iron canister.

As Scooter knelt at her side, she removed the delicate paper. The map showed an intricate system of pathways. They stared at the unfamiliar landmarks and coded language, but neither of them could decipher any of it.

"It probably won't make sense until we have the other two maps," Scooter resolved.

"You should've grabbed them from the skeleton like I told you to," Stokely prodded.

"I didn't have time! Cricklewood and Silas would've seen me. We'll get the maps when we go back," Scooter replied. "Just read me that little stanza thing one more time."

Stokely squinted her eyes and peered closely at the peculiar calligraphy on the top right corner of the map.

She read the words:

Place twin hands,
On the Golden Door,
And find yourself
On the crypt floor.

"The crypt floor," Scooter repeated. "It has to have something to do with what Mayor Waddletub and Fink were talking about on the night of the Star Festival. Winky said that Tripper reported the Black Candle missing from a *crypt*. And Tripper said something 'bout a crypt when we were camping. Maybe it's the same place."

"One thing's for sure. We need to get back inside the tower," Stokely said. "We'll never figure anything out just sitting around here."

"I don't know if you remember, but every time we go out there, something terrible happens."

Before Scooter and Stokely could discuss the map any further, a heavy hand knocked on the outhouse door.

"Hello?" Gabbo called. "Anyone in there?"

Stokely quickly crammed the map into the box, and kicked dirt over the secret hideaway.

Scooter opened the outhouse door to see his father, covered in dirt just as he was every evening after a long day's work.

"Why, hello Pa," Scooter said casually. "We were just playing hide and seek, and I found Stokely in here."

"Glad you found her. Because Twilly Deathglow has sent a dozen letters to our breezebox in the last hour, all requesting pumpkins," Gabbo said. "I know it's gettin' late, but I need you to take a wagonload over to her place. As you know, it's been a tough October for the pumpkin business, and this is the biggest order we've had all month."

"Sure, Pa, we'll take care of it," Stokely replied.

Scooter and Stokely ran out of the outhouse toward the wagon. Its bed was already filled with a mound of the choicest crop. Two mules stood hitched to the squeaky cart. Hotchkiss, the family dog, ran to join the twins so he would not be left to roam the haunted fields alone. The trio jumped up onto the driver's perch, and Stokely commanded the reins. She slapped the mules' backs, and the wagon tussled forward.

But just before they sped away, Gabbo waved for them to stop.

"By the way, if you see any of your brothers and sisters, tell them to come home immediately. Your Ma is worried sick. They left the house this morning, but we haven't seen them since. Last we heard, they were going back to Gubbles' Goodies for a taste of that new brew everyone's been talking about. Also, Tripper Boneglaze was by the farm this afternoon. Said he'd like a private word with the two of you. Said it was urgent."

Chapter 21:

A Strange Game

"**W**hy do you think Tripper wants to see us?" Stokely asked Scooter as the pumpkin wagon rolled over the East Bridge and in to Town Square.

Scooter thought for a moment before he responded, "Don't know. But I'd hate to get a warning when it's already too late."

When they arrived in Town Square, the streets and shops were quiet and dark. A woman's lone song echoed out of the purple doorway and into the empty, lamp-lit streets. The wagon groaned as it rolled to a slow stop in front of Gubbles' Goodies.

"Let's stop in here before we make the delivery. The Gubble sisters may know something about Milky and Rudd and all the others," Stokely said.

The twins walked into the shop, and Hotchkiss followed right behind.

Gertrude Gubble stood alone behind the service counter, singing the sweet melody as she poured a sack of colored powder into a giant, black cauldron.

"Excuse me," Stokely interrupted.

The shopkeeper turned, and smiled in delight at the sight of her latest customers.

"Hello children! You're out late tonight," Gertrude trilled, wiping her powdery hands on her apron. "I don't recognize your precious faces, darlings. You mustn't have tasted the new brew yet, hmm? Here, have a taste or two."

Gertrude held out a wooden spoon full of the bubbling liquid.

"No thanks," Stokely replied. "We're in a hurry. We just have a few questions."

"Very well. But let's make a game of it, shall we? For every answer I give, you must sip a spoonful of the brew," Gertrude chirped.

"Okay," Scooter answered. "My Pa told us our brothers and sisters came in here today, but no one has seen them since. Maybe you saw 'em earlier? There'd be ten all together. Dirty feet and overalls. Prolly smelled like the creek too."

"Oh my," Gertrude replied with heartfelt concern. "I'm sorry to say I haven't seen your brothers and sisters today. They've never come into the bakery."

Scooter and Stokely looked at one another in confusion.

Gertrude exclaimed, "You must be the Scabbins twins!"

"That's right," Stokely answered. "If it's not too much trouble, I'd like to speak with Plumb. Do you know where we can find her?"

"Our Auntie Plumb has been sick all month. She's asleep upstairs, and has asked not to be bothered by visitors," Gertrude replied. "Now, I answered two questions, so each of you must take a spoonful! A deal is a deal!"

Gertrude spun towards the cauldron and dipped two wooden spoons into the bubbling liquid. But when she turned back around, the Scabbins twins and their dog were already gone.

"Shame, shame," the beautiful woman said. "I didn't even have the chance to tell them that Professor Boneglaze was in here this evening asking all about them. Never seen a man in such a fright."

Scooter knocked on the door of Twilly Deathglow's pumpkin carving shop, Jack Of All Lanterns, and waited for the old maid to answer.

After a few moments, the screen door swung open, revealing a woman with white streaks running through her massive tangle of black hair. Long feathered earrings hung down to her shoulders.

"You two owe me a bucket of nails," Twilly croaked with a slight grin. "Me outhouse fell to the ground last Monday. I know you'se are the ones 'ta stoled 'em."

"Don't have a notion of what you're talking about, Miss Deathglow," Stokely said, averting Twilly's penetrating gaze. "Where should we put the pumpkins?"

"Go'se up the stairs and out 'ta the balcony," Twilly said, pointing to a slanted staircase in her shop.

The twins hauled the pumpkins, one by one, up to the outdoor balcony, and piled them in the corner. From the view of the balcony, the twins could see a curtained, upstairs window above the bakery next door. The window was dark, but a faint light fluttered from within.

"I'll bet Plumb's in there now," Scooter whispered into the night. "It's a shame she's so sick."

"Something's fishy with that. Plumb wouldn't mind if we visited her for just a minute or two—even if she wasn't feeling swell. I mean, we've known her our whole lives," Stokely said. "Come on, I have an idea."

Stokely jumped over the balcony and landed on Twilly's shingled roof. Scooter sighed and followed after his intrepid sister. The two scrambled across the rooftop and leapt across the narrow alleyway onto the roof of Gubbles' Goodies. They were careful not to be heard in the bakery below as they snuck across the rooftop shingles to the curtained window.

Scooter used the cuff of his shirt to wipe two circular clearings in the soot of the window. The twins pressed their faces to the window, and looked into a room lit by a single, flickering candle. Glass jars lined the walls, and empty ones were scattered all over the floor.

And there, lying on her bed, hands and feet bound to the bedposts, and a bright red rag stuffed in her mouth, was Plumb.

Chapter 22:

A Child Without Spirit

On the night of Hallows Eve, Gabbo and Rose Scabbins sat in their rocking chairs by the roaring fire, worried sick about their missing children. Like so many other Hobblers, they watched the latest broadcast of the Monster Watch, tensely awaiting the addition of their children's names to the growing list of vanishings.

Things had been made even worse the night before, when Deputy Notwod escorted Scooter and Stokely back home and told Gabbo that his two eldest children were spreading dangerous rumors around Hobble, stirring up fear in everyone who lent an ear to their ludicrous stories. First, it was the letters about a Vothlor prisoner being alive and loose, and killing Pappy Cricklewood. Then, the twins had awoken Deputy, screaming insanities about Plumb being tied up and held captive by the Gubbles. Deputy had checked on Plumb, but found her asleep, just as the Gubbles had said. He then threatened to lock up the Scabbins twins if they continued with such fictions.

"We can't tolerate this kind of fear-mongering," Deputy Notwod had argued to Gabbo. "If they keep stirring up fear, then the nightmares will infect us all."

Scooter and Stokely walked into their firelit den dressed in their traditional Hallows Eve costumes—white ghost-sheets with holes cut out for the eyes and mouth. Both of the twins held empty candy buckets in their hands.

"We're going trick or treating," Scooter announced. "Won't be back 'til late."

Rose looked upon her two eldest children with sad, red-rimmed eyes.

"It's not safe this October, my darlings," she explained. "Perhaps next October things will be merry once again."

Gabbo pulled himself up from his rocking chair, and turned off the Hobble Tube. The farmer paced back and forth in the den, mulling over Scooter and Stokely's proposition. He fondly thought back to his own rambunctious childhood days of smashing pumpkins on porches and raiding candy cauldrons.

Gabbo finally turned to his wife and said, "No family of mine will be crippled by fear. What do you say, Rose?"

Rose closed her eyes, took a deep breath, and nodded her head.

"You're right, Gabbo. A child without spirit is no child at all." The rosy-cheeked woman turned to face Scooter and Stokely. "Just promise you won't allow yourselves to be separated."

Stokely and Scooter placed their hands over their hearts and promised. Then they ran out of the Pumpkin House, down the front steps, and toward Town Square. But once they were hidden within the woods of Midnight Creek, they shed their ghost-sheets, and changed direction.

They scampered back toward the Forbidden Watchtower looming upon the northeastern horizon—to fetch the other two maps.

Scooter and Stokely rowed across the swamp in C.C. Pottleman's boat, which they had kept forgetting to return.

"Okay, so Tripper must have been looking for us because he knew we were near the swamp. He is a Spymaster, after all. Probably knows we have this map, too. He must want to warn us about it for one reason or another," Scooter said as they paddled across the calm water.

"But warn us about what?"

"Nittle, maybe? Or maybe he wanted to warn us to quit being fools and stop comin' to a haunted watchtower in the middle of the night."

"Don't worry. We'll be alright. Just gotta stick together," Stokely assured, noticing her brother's concern. "Remember what the Tree Of Memories said?"

The twins circled around the tower to the hidden staircase, and climbed to the top floor. Moonlight poured into the room from a dozen tiny windows, casting strange shadows.

Stokely used their two flint rocks to light a nearby torch on fire. With the torch as their guide, the twins made their way to the chamber with the skeleton.

"Let's just get the maps and get out of here. Silas said Malivar's whispers have been here several times this month," Scooter said, frightened by the prospect of meeting the dark vapor. "We'll figure out the maps when we get back home."

Stokely lifted the torch so her brother could grab the maps.

But only a pouch of marbles lay where the maps had been.

Chapter 23:

The Cobwebbed Door

"**S**omeone stole the other two maps!" Scooter whispered, his face pale. "It must have been Silas—or—or Malivar! *He* knows. You said your name was scratched into that marble pouch? Malivar knows it's us who has the other map, Stokely."

Scooter began to pace the room, recalling the nightmare he had seen in the Lostwood.

It all makes sense now, he thought.

"If he knows it's us, what's to stop him from coming right up to our front door?! Nittle had one of your marbles, too! They *all* know, Stokely. All the Vothlor know we're snoopin' around. That's what Tripper wanted to warn us about. We have to get out of here *right now*!"

"You should've grabbed the other maps when I told you to!" Stokely accused.

Scooter opened the cylinder and removed the lone map.

"Tripper said the Vothlor are looking for these maps. As long as we have this one, they'll be coming for us," he said, examining the lines and markings of the scroll for the hundredth time. Scooter pointed at the skeleton slumped beside the cobwebbed door. "They probably found out this man had the maps and killed him for it!"

"But why wouldn't they have just taken them when they killed him, instead of leaving the maps here with his skeleton? Maybe they didn't know he had them, or didn't know what they were? Besides, if he had the maps the Vothlor were lookin' for, why would he bring them here?" Stokely asked, looking at the direction the skeleton had been walking when he must have died.

Stokely walked over to the door and began tearing away the thick layers of spiderwebs. Hairy arachnids fled into cracks in the walls, and a cloud of dust filled the doorway. Stokely searched for a handle, and shoved with all her might, but the door would not budge.

"My turn," Scooter said, and began a more meticulous examination of the portal.

He found a crooked slot in the middle of the door.

"We need some kind of key. There's no other way to open it. No handle. Nothing," he said.

"Maybe the skeleton wanted to get to the other side of this door. Check his pockets. Maybe he had the key before—before he turned into a skeleton," Stokely suggested.

Scooter rummaged through the dead man's pockets, but found nothing.

Stokely examined the door. She scraped her fingers through the silky cobwebs, and saw a golden hue shimmering along the thin finger-marks she had carved.

"Scooter, you better come take a look at this," Stokely said.

Scooter walked over to the cobwebbed door and gazed upon it in admiration.

"This door is gold!" he shouted.

"Look at the map again!" Stokely said with excitement. "Read the directions."

Scooter took out the fragile document and turned it upside-down so they could read the strange stanza.

Place twin hands
On the Golden Door,
To find yourself
On the crypt floor.

Stokely looked up at her brother with a bright smile.

Suddenly, footsteps plodded down a nearby hallway—familiar footsteps.

"Malivar," Scooter whispered, the blood drained from his face. "We better get a move on!"

"Quick, Scooter! Put your hands on the door!"

Scooter and Stokely each placed one hand on the Golden Door, and leaned against it. As Scooter looked over his shoulder in a fright, the footsteps drew nearer, and a sharp whisper invaded the chamber.

Scooter panicked.

"It's not gonna work, Stoke—"

But before he could finish his sentence, the floor beneath their feet gave way and the twins tumbled headfirst through a trapdoor.

Chapter 24:

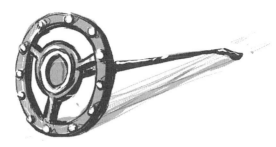

The Watchtower Secret

Scooter screamed at the top of his lungs as the twins slid . . . and slid . . . and slid down a steep, smooth slope, finally landing on a pile of potato sacks stuffed with straw.

Scooter groaned and stood to his feet, while Stokely re-lit the torch with her flint rocks. They could still hear the strange moan coming from above. When Scooter looked up at the ceiling, he saw a metal fan whirling wildly and blowing into a glass funnel. It was this vortex of air blowing through the funnel that created the strange, moaning sound, which traveled through several vents leading into the Forbidden Watchtower. When the air whipped through the vents, it moved pairs of wooden clogs to create a tapping sound, like the sound of shoes walking on stones.

"It's all a hoax," Scooter realized. "Just a trick to keep people away! This watchtower isn't haunted at all."

His sister did not respond.

"Did you hear me, Stokely? We've been duped. The

whole town's been duped. The Forbidden Watchtower's not haunted! It all comes from these ancient rigs. I bet ole Cricklewood wanted to keep people from figuring out that the Vothlor prisoner was up there."

"Scoot, I think I know another reason why," Stokely finally spoke.

Scooter turned around to see his sister spinning in a slow circle, staring at the room in awe. Strange symbols covered the walls. But one symbol in the chamber was far larger than the rest: a circle with twelve dots surrounding it, like the numbers of a clock. Scooter and Stokely looked down at the floor, and examined the symbol painted onto the enormous stone tiles. The room was circular, and twelve tall doorways were spread evenly along the walls. Each of the doors lined up with one of the dots on the floor.

"We've seen this symbol everywhere," Stokely said, walking around the room. "Wonder what it means."

She walked to a bin next to a cold hearth. Inside the bin was a long metal rod with the symbol shaped onto its end. The symbol was charred with ash.

"It's a branding iron," Scooter said from across the room. "They're used to sear symbols onto cows or goats to mark who owns them. Can't imagine that any cows or goats have been down here, though, and I ain't never seen that symbol on the back side of a heifer."

Stokely tossed the branding iron back into the bin next to the hearth.

"I think—I think this must be the crypt that Winky and Fink were talking about on the night of the Star Festival. Don't you see how it's all connected, Scoot? The Black Candle, the murders, the Forbidden Watchtower, this map. This is the secret crypt where the Black Candle was sealed away!"

Stokely waved her torch toward the darkness.

At the entrance to one of the passageways, there was a bloodstained ¥ painted onto the wall.

"The mark of the Vothlor," Stokely said. "That must be the chamber where the Black Candle was kept. Come on Scoot, let's find a way out of here. This place gives me the creeps."

Scooter quickly scanned the map and pointed to a circle with twelve lines extending from it, in the same layout as the symbol on the walls and floor.

"Look! You can see this room and the twelve doors right here! Each of the doors is a new tunnel or passageway. We're at the center of it all."

Stokely leaned in and peered at the map.

"I'll bet that hallway leads back to Town Square," Scooter said, pointing to the southwestern tunnel. He held up the map and turned it to make sure his hypothesis was correct. "Hey, look, here's a pathway down here that breaks away from the main tunnel. Looks like a shortcut."

Scooter held the map in front of him as he led the way through the tunnel.

Stokely followed close behind with the torch, admiring the strange and wonderful art which adorned the walls of the tunnels. She wondered if the secret knowledge of the tunnels' location had died along with the earlier generations of Hobblers who had built them, or if any Hobblers still knew about the underground passageways.

After a few minutes, Scooter stopped again and peered

down at the map. He shook his head and quickly turned around.

"If the map's true, the door to the shortcut should be right here," he mused aloud, turning to face a solid stone wall.

Scooter pounded his fists against the stone, and a deep, hollow sound echoed on the other side. He looked down and noticed a handle at the bottom of the wall.

As he turned the lever, the stone wall slowly rumbled upwards, revealing a pathway which looked far more rugged and dangerous than the main tunnels.

"You sure this is a shortcut?" Stokely whispered. She held the torch out, and stepped across the threshold.

"I'm not sure of anything tonight," Scooter said as he followed his sister into the darkness.

Chapter 25:

Table Of Death

Stokely reached for her pocketknife, and flipped open the small blade to defend herself from whatever creatures lay waiting in the unseen caverns ahead.

"What does the map show?" she asked Scooter, as two rats scurried across the pool of torchlight and vanished into the blackness.

Scooter looked down at the map to determine their location.

"We're *here*, but there's no tellin' where it leads," Scooter whispered, tracing his dirty finger across the map. The line stopped short of a small, golden circle.

"What's that?" Stokely asked.

"It looks like some kind of coin. If this is the crypt where the Black Candle was hidden, maybe it means treasure. Remember what Winky and Tripper said about other treasures being down here? 'Great and terrible things,' they said."

Stokely squared her shoulders and stepped further into the darkness.

The twins followed along a winding tunnel, squeezing through small crevices and ducking beneath low overhangs.

"Scoot, I found something!" Stokely announced.

She held the torch up to illuminate a split in the passageway. An old wooden sign was planted in the ground between the two tunnels, and pointed to the left. It read:

TO THE MINISTRY

Strangely, no arrow pointed the other direction to where the coin was located on the map.

"There must be an exit near the Ministry Of Light," Scooter said. "Director Stevens could maybe help us out, if he's not still mad about us releasing those snakes during his service last month."

Scooter looked down the western tunnel, which somehow seemed darker than the one leading back to Town Square.

A flash of pale light materialized in the darkness, and Scooter took a step backwards.

"Hello?" he whispered.

A girl wearing a blue gown stood in the middle of the dark passageway, opposite the one leading to the Ministry. The girl tilted her head and smiled at Scooter and Stokely, but said nothing. Finally, she giggled and motioned for the twins to follow her into the darkness.

"Tell me you see that girl," Scooter said.

"Come on, Scoot. I think—I think she's trying to help us," Stokely replied.

"What if she isn't? What if we're in a nightmare right now? What is she doing down here, anyway? I don't recognize her from town."

The girl began to hum an eerie tune as she walked farther into the darkness. The tail of her blue gown could be seen at the edge of the torchlight.

"Come along, come along . . ." the girl's tender voice whispered.

Stokely looked at her brother and said, "What have we got to lose?"

"Other than our lives, nothing," Scooter conceded. "You go first."

The twisting, underground hall grew narrower until two boulders blocked the twins from going any further—but the strange girl was nowhere to be seen.

"Okay, I guess now we go back," Scooter said.

Ignoring her brother, Stokely squeezed through a small crevice. Scooter shook his head and followed.

On the other side of the boulders, Stokely held the torch out into the darkness. Immediately, the twins recoiled in fright.

Four skeletons sat in wooden chairs around a stone table, their hollow eyes staring back at the twins. Shreds of clothing clung to the skeletons' exposed ribcages and they wore leather boots on their bony feet.

"Come on, we've gone this far," Stokely whispered, stepping through the opening and into the skeleton room.

As soon as they both stepped into the room, the boulders rumbled together behind them, sealing them into the chamber.

Chapter 26:

The Key To The Omni

Stokely began to shove against the stones.

"It's no use," Scooter replied from behind her, his chest heaving in fright. "It's a trap. We couldn't move those boulders in a hundred years."

Stokely hung her head and turned around.

"So what now? We just die in here like *them*?" she said. Mice ran in and out of the skeletons' bones, and cobwebs stretched from one empty eye socket to another.

"We're inside another nightmare," Scooter declared. "It's him. It's Malivar. He's in our heads."

"Don't be such a scaredy-cat, Scoot," Stokely announced curtly. "This ain't no nightmare. Besides, it's just some skeletons. I don't think they're goin' anywhere anytime soon."

She reached out to touch one of the skeletons.

"Don't!" Scooter yelped. "It's bad luck to disturb the dead."

The farm boy carefully walked to the other side of the table and found four swords lying beneath a blanket against the furthest wall. The hilts of the swords bore the symbol of the circle with twelve dots.

"I think these guys were here to protect something," Scooter said, lifting one of the heavy, metal swords for Stokely to see. "They're dressed like warriors from the Old War."

"They should have sent down some replacements," Stokely quipped.

"Maybe the replacements couldn't find this place," Scooter answered. "I mean, without the map, we never would have wound up in this room."

As the twins surveyed the warrior skeletons, they both took notice of a small wooden box resting on the center of the table. The Sacred Circle was imprinted onto the middle of the box, just above two slots. The box was attached to the table and was scratched badly, as if someone had tried to tear it open a hundred times before, but to no avail.

"See if it's unlocked," Stokely dared.

"I doubt it," Scooter answered. "If it was unlocked, then I'm sure whatever was inside has long been stolen. The Vothlor would have taken anything valuable, along with the Black Candle."

Scooter took a few steps closer, until he was right alongside the table. He slowly reached out and touched the box. As soon as Scooter's hand grazed it, all four skeletons stood up from their chairs, drew long spears, and pointed them at the twins.

"They're alive!" Scooter shrieked.

He stumbled backwards as he and Stokely scrambled

out of the spears' reach.

The skeletons were protecting the box through some kind of magic.

"They don't want us to touch the box," Scooter said, out of breath.

"Maybe not, but maybe there's something inside that can help us. After all, the box has the mark of the Armiji—and they're the good guys."

"After you," Scooter dared, motioning Stokely to lead the way.

The four skeletons faced the girl as she approached the box. Blood pulsed in her ears, and her palms became sweaty.

She glanced down at the box, examined it, and smiled.

"Give me your flint rock," she said, removing the stone from around her neck.

"My flint rock?"

"Just trust me."

Scooter tossed the rock to his sister. She held the rocks side by side, right next to the two slots in the box.

"You sure that's going to work?" Scooter asked, looking up at the four warriors ready to attack. "This isn't like the door to Fink's cottage. I don't think that's the kind of lock you can pick with a couple of dull rocks."

"I don't need to pick the lock. These are the keys to the lock."

Without a moment of doubt, Stokely inserted the two flint rocks into the slots, and turned them.

Suddenly, glowing words appeared on top of the box, coiling like a snake around the Sacred Circle symbol.

I am greater than the Light and
more evil than the Darkness.
The poorest Hobblers have me,
and the richest Hobblers need me.
If you eat me, you will die.
What am I?

Whisper the answer into the keyhole.
If you are wrong, you will die.

"The flint rocks. The riddle. Tripper must have known we would be here!" Scooter mused. "He was preparing us for this moment. But why?"

"It doesn't matter," Stokely answered. "Right now, we need to figure out this riddle, or else we're gonna die."

Scooter paced around the room, mumbling to himself all of the incorrect answers he had considered since Tripper first proposed the riddle.

"Just take it one line at a time," Stokely suggested.

"Leave the riddle to me," Scooter replied, scratching his chin. "Greater than the Light. More evil than . . . the poorest . . . the richest . . . eat me, you'll die. It could be anything!" Scooter mumbled to himself.

Stokely walked over to the box and looked down at the riddle.

"One line at a time," she whispered.

What is greater than the Light? she read.

Stokely's eyes immediately lit up, and a smile curled upon her lips.

"*Nothing,*" she whispered into the keyhole of the box.

Immediately, the skeletons withdrew their spears and

sat back down. The box clicked open, and Scooter turned in astonishment.

"How—" he began.

"The answer is *nothing*," Stokely replied with a smile. "Nothing is greater than the Light. Nothing is more evil than the Darkness. The poor have nothing. The rich need nothing. And if you eat nothing, you'll die!"

Stokely patted her brother's back, and he looked back at her with dazed admiration.

"Now, let's see what's inside," Stokely whispered. A musty scent arose from within the box.

She cautiously reached her hand inside, and lifted out a large, iron key. Next, she removed a delicate piece of yellowed paper, written in the same calligraphic handwriting as the riddles.

Stokely cleared her throat and read the inscription aloud, "*Beware. You now hold the key to the Omni. . .* why does that sound so familiar?"

"I think Silas might have mentioned it to Pappy," Scooter replied. "Said it had been hidden from the Vothlor to protect its powers."

"Come on, let's get back home," Stokely said. "We'll show this key to Pa, and he can take it to the Elders. Whatever this is, it must be important."

Just before the twins exited the room, Scooter noticed something in the corner.

A child's skeleton lay crumpled on the floor. He walked closer for a better look, and his blood ran cold.

The skeleton wore a blue gown, and a flint rock necklace hung around its neck.

Chapter 27:

SILAS CRITCHFIELD

Ministry Of Darkness

Scooter and Stokely squeezed through the small crevice between the two giant rocks. Stokely ran to the end of the hallway and waited for Scooter to catch up.

"We have to figure out how to get out of these tunnels," she said. "Or we're going to wind up just like that ghost girl in the blue dress."

Stokely shivered as they followed the pathway back to the place where they had seen the sign leading to the Ministry.

"This should lead us back toward Town Square," Scooter said.

The twins ran close together, ducking beneath low overhangs and leaping over collapsed sections of the tunnel.

Finally, they saw a great, purple glow emanating into the darkness of the tunnels.

"Is that the Ministry?" Stokely asked.

Scooter glanced at the map and nodded. "Maybe Director Stevens is in there now. We could send him for help."

They arrived at an entrance into a magnificent room with vaulted ceilings. A long table stretched through the middle of the room, where the purple glow seemed to be fading into darkness, as if a candle had left some light behind. In all of their trips to the Ministry Of Light, they had never seen this room.

"Smells like fireworks down here," Stokely noticed, sniffing the smoky air.

"What is this place?" Scooter asked. The boy felt the presence of something evil in their midst. Then, he noticed a photograph hanging on the wall and nudged his sister. "Over there. Look familiar?"

Stokely looked across the room to see an exact likeness of the prisoner from the watchtower—the same one Pappy Cricklewood set free.

"Silas?" Stokely realized, glancing around the chamber. "This is the same place from the photo we saw in Fink's house. Look at the table. Silas must have closed up this room after he betrayed Hobble."

A familiar voice interrupted the twins, "Ah, but *betrayed* is such a dirty word."

Scooter and Stokely whipped their heads around to see Nittle Nightbrook. She was already moving towards them.

"After all, one day you will be the ones seen as traitors, and I will be seen as a loyal servant to Malivar. Of course, you'll be long dead by then."

Scooter and Stokely cowered backwards into a corner.

Nittle held a slight smile as she closed in on them. "You're too late. You've just missed him. He was here, not ten minutes ago. Sadly, our ceremony was interrupted by a rotten, stinking boy. The stupid Director's son."

Starflyer knows about all of this, too? Scooter questioned. *I hope he's okay.*

Nittle pressed the twins into the corner and spread her arms wide to keep them from running anywhere. When Stokely tried to escape, Nittle squeezed her throat and threw her into the damp stone wall. She had unbelievable strength, as if empowered by something beyond herself.

"I suppose you should be congratulated," Nittle continued, reaching into a pocket of her dress. "You've done a fine job sniffing out clues. Too bad your little adventure has to come to an end."

She revealed a gleaming pair of pliers and pressed both twins into the corner.

"You won't be doing any more sniffing around once I've ripped off your noses!"

Nittle opened the pliers and closed them onto Stokely's nose. The librarian began to cackle madly, and hissed at Stokely.

Just as she was about to twist the pliers, Nittle's face jerked into a shock. Her mouth hung open, and her arms fell to her side. She began to groan, and a slight trickle of blood ran from her nose.

She collapsed to her knees, and fell over, dead.

Fink Karbunkle stood behind her, holding his hatchet.

111

Chapter 28:

Familiar Voices

"**F**ink!" Stokely cried out.

Fink dropped his hatchet in horror.

"I—I'm so sorry, children," Fink cried. "I'm no murderer, but I couldn't let her hurt you. I just couldn't allow it."

Stokely ran to Fink's side, and hugged him.

"You saved our lives," Scooter said. He reached out and shook Fink's wrinkled hand.

"I suppose I did," Fink answered. He took a deep breath and looked at Nittle lying on the ground, dead. "I've been pretending to be a Vothlor all month long. With my reputation, it wasn't difficult to convince them to trust me. I never told the Elders about it, because they'd believe I had really joined. I was told there was to be a meeting here tonight, and I planned to find out what Malivar was up to this time. I came in late, and that's when I saw Miss Nightbrook leaning over the two of you. She would have killed you, too. Know that this is no game, children. A new war has begun."

Fink glanced over at the image of Silas hanging on the wall and hung his head.

"Whatever they say about me, children, know that I'm as loyal to Hobble as any other. I've made mistakes—some more terrible than others—but I'll never *really* join the Vothlor again."

Scooter and Stokely nodded.

"So, what do we do now?" Stokely asked.

"Stay hidden!" Fink warned. "Hide in the tunnels until daybreak. Malivar is on the move, and I fear his secret vessel is about to do something terrible. No one knows who it is—not even the members of the meeting tonight. I'd hate to see you two caught up in whatever nightmares Malivar has planned. I'll fetch Orson Stevens Jr., and let him know what happened. Now, off with you!"

Scooter and Stokely ran out of the Ministry and back into the tunnels, with Nittle Nightbrook's blood on the bottom of their shoes.

"We could go back to the crypt until morning," Stokely suggested. "Come on. I think I remember how to get back."

"Shh!" Scooter whispered. "You hear that?"

Far away, they heard men's voices echoing from the tunnels.

The voices grew louder as Scooter and Stokely followed the prints into the deep darkness.

"Snuff the torch," Scooter whispered.

Stokely pressed the end of the torch into the ground to

kill the flame. She reached out and grabbed hold of Scooter's shirt so they would not be separated. Up ahead was a glow of torchlight. Scooter and Stokely felt their way along the dirt walls and stopped at the next bend.

The twins peeked around the corner into the room with the two men. One had his back to the twins and wore a cloak, so they could not be sure who he was.

But the second was Tripper Boneglaze.

Chapter 29

Traitors To Hobble

Scooter and Stokely ducked into the shadows, and cupped their hands over their mouths to muffle their breathing. The two men stood only a few feet from them.

"Well?" the cloaked man asked. "What news have you?"

"I've seen them just now," Tripper answered. "Headed right this way."

"Were they alone?" the other man asked, stepping towards Tripper.

"No. They had one more. Twined up in another potato sack."

"Going in what direction?" the veiled figure asked.

"East, toward the mines."

Scooter and Stokely leaned forward from their hiding place so they could hear the conversation more clearly.

"It seems they've been true to their word," the cloaked

man whispered.

"Everything is in place. This night will be a great success in pursuit of our cause. All of our lies to the Hobblers will come to fruition on this night."

Lies to the Hobblers? Stokely questioned. *What has Tripper been lying about? Did he lie to us, too?*

"I have more news. Unexpected news," Tripper added. "It seems the prisoner has escaped from the tower. I found this in the tunnels."

The schoolteacher held up a black playing card—a cloaked vapor appeared in all four corners of the card.

The other man snatched the card and quickly tucked it into his cloak.

"Cricklewood!" he whispered. "No other had the power to release Silas. Alas, this may work out even better than we dreamed."

Scooter and Stokely mouthed the word to one another, *Vothlor.* They could not believe their own mentor, the very person who invited them to join the Spymasters, was working for the other side. Maybe Crook Wigglesworth had been right—*no one could be trusted.*

"Now, to the matter of the relics in the crypt. Will it be difficult to acquire them?" Tripper asked.

"Yes."

"Are you certain?" Tripper asked.

"The Black Candle has been taken, yes. But the other secrets will be more difficult to obtain. The key to the Omni is out of reach for now," the other man replied. "Strange magic has been cast upon its skeleton protectors. The box cannot be opened."

Scooter and Stokely glanced at one another. The man's

voice was familiar, but they could not place it. Scooter reached into his pocket and rubbed the iron key they had won from the wooden box in the crypt. Somehow, it felt heavier than it had only moments before.

The man continued, "Even if someone found a way into the crypt, they would need the Omni to find their way out of the tunnels, or to any of the other relics. That map had to have been destroyed during the Old War—if not a hundred years ago during the Gold Crusades. So, take heart. Everything is going according to the plan."

"I simply don't trust others being down here," Tripper said. "Everything we have worked so hard to protect is now vulnerable. You forget how powerful they are, especially when together. If they were to somehow acquire the key to the Omni, then we would have no way to stop them."

"You, above all, know how difficult that prospect will be," the man replied.

Tripper's face dimmed with sadness. He reached up to his neck, where the flint-rock necklace hung like a heavy weight.

Tripper had a twin sister, Scooter realized. *The ghost girl in the blue gown.*

The shadowed man placed his pruned hand on Tripper's shoulder and said, "If all goes as planned, Hobble's destiny will be rewritten tonight. We will change the course of our history."

Tripper nodded. "You've done all that's necessary to carry out our plot, and Hobblers will never know you were the one behind it all. It's amazing how they've believed every word you've ever told them."

The man nodded and replied, "The fates are aligning.

Malivar walks free."

The shadowed figure turned his face into the torchlight.
Scooter and Stokely's mouths fell open in disbelief.
There, alive and well, was Mayor Winky Waddletub.

Chapter 30:

Three For The Gallows

Right then, a trio of women's voices echoed through the tunnels.

Tripper and Winky turned toward the sound.

"So it begins," Winky whispered. "Come along. We'll wait in the crypt until this night has passed."

Tripper and Winky stepped past the twins without noticing their presence. The two conspirators' voices faded as they moved away.

Scooter and Stokely waited until the torchlight was out of sight, and when the passage was clear, they began to chatter about all they had just witnessed. Winky Waddletub was alive! And he and Tripper were somehow involved in the wicked plots of the Vothlor.

"What should we do now?" Stokely whispered.

Scooter lifted the Omni-key out of his pocket and gripped the cold metal within his sweaty palm.

"You heard what they said," he replied. "This key has some kind of special power. So whatever's behind the door it opens must be pretty important."

After Stokely re-lit the torch, Scooter took out the map and studied the maze of tunnels. If the map proved correct, there was an exit somewhere ahead, right beneath Town Square. It was the same direction from which those female voices had come a few minutes before.

"Let's go this way," Scooter said, pointing southwest.

"You sure?" Stokely challenged.

"They're going to come looking for us when they find out the key to the Omni is gone. And if this key is as important as they say, and it's been protected for a hundred years, then we don't want it to fall into their hands. Fink was right to suspect the mayor on the night of the Star Festival. Winky and Tripper have been hiding something from all of us. Hate to say it, but I think they're part of the Vothlor—maybe even the secret Hobbler that Crook was talkin' about. For now, you and me can only trust each other. We need to hustle it back to town and find Pa. Hopefully Fink has already gathered up a posse."

They had not taken a dozen steps down the tunnel when they heard the sounds of shoes tapping against the stone walkway. Scooter quickly studied the map, and snuffed the torch again.

The twins looked for the source of the women's voices. A single lantern dangled in the darkness.

Scooter and Stokely watched in amazement as the three Gubble sisters came into view, their faces stern and determined—a sharp contrast to the masks of merriment they had worn all month in the bakery. They also carried a large sack.

"Get down!" Scooter whispered to Stokely.

The twins lay flat on the cold ground in the intersecting passageway, and held their breaths. The Gubbles' boots tapped along the stone floor of the passageway as the three women passed by.

Gertrude Gubble patted the sack and announced, "We're lucky to have found this one. I wonder what he was doing wondering around the alleyways outside the Ministry."

Darkness flooded back over Scooter and Stokely as the Gubbles moved farther away.

The twins then heard something they wished was not real. A boy's frightened voice whimpered from within the sack. Issa knocked her club over the head of the sack and the captive quieted.

"There's someone in that bag! We can't let the Gubbles get away!" Stokely declared. "Let's get to Town Square and gather everyone we can trust. It seems there's more people working for the Vothlor than we ever could have imagined. Saving the kids comes first. Remember what Fink said about Malivar? The dark vapor can only be conjured back from the void on Hallows Eve. What if Malivar's already been resurrected tonight? I'd hate for something to happen like in the Old War, when all those kids disappeared and were said to have been murdered. We'll hunt down the Gubbles before midnight and send them to the gallows where they belong."

"No," Scooter argued. "We should follow them. We can't risk losing their trail."

Stokely thought for a moment and confidently replied,

"I'll go for help, and you follow after the Gubbles. Stay far behind them so they don't see or hear you. I'll gather Pa and the other farmers, and we'll come find you."

"How you going to get out of here?" Scooter questioned.

"I'm guessing the Gubbles came from Town Square. I'll head that way and see what I can find."

Stokely turned to run into the darkness of the tunnel, but Scooter caught her arm.

He whispered, "Wait a minute. The Tree Of Memories told us to never separate. And Ma made us promise her we'd stay together tonight. We're strongest when we're together. I say we *both* go for help, or we *both* stay down here and follow the Gubbles together."

"It doesn't matter anymore what Tripper or the Tree Of Memories said," Stokely insisted. "It makes more sense for me to gather up some Hobblers, and you track down the Gubbles before they can hurt anyone else. We'll have a better chance of saving the kids if we do it this way. I'll even leave the torch with you. Town Square can't be far from here." She reached into her pocket, and pulled out one of her mother's biscuits leftover from dinner. "Here, take this biscuit and leave a trail of breadcrumbs for me and the posse to follow."

"But, Stokely—" Scooter pleaded.

Stokely patted her brother's shoulder, and turned to run down the cold, silent tunnel. She estimated Town Square was no more than a quarter mile ahead, and she was certain she would find a ladder or tunnel leading back up to Hobble.

She ran ahead with utmost confidence in her plan.

Until she heard Scooter scream at the top of his lungs, pleading for his life.

Chapter 31:

This Night Has Only Just Begun

Stokely whirled around and raced toward where Scooter's cries reverberated off the stone walls.

Just ahead, Scooter lay on the floor of the tunnel, held down by Vivy and Gertrude Gubble. He was trying to kick himself free, but the sisters pressed their knees into his shoulders. Issa Gubble loomed over the boy with her hands resting on her hips.

"Lemme go, you hussies!" Scooter demanded. "I swear you'll meet the gallows before this night is over!"

"I don't think so, boy," Issa said calmly. "For us, this night has only just begun. We have many things still to do, and you're coming with us. Just like *him*."

She nodded toward the sack. Vivy slightly opened the bag to reveal a glimpse of the sleeping boy within. Behind the green lenses of a peculiar pair of goggles, Starflyer Stevens' eyes were open, but unseeing. The young captive appeared to be imprisoned by some kind of magical trance.

His skin glistened, as if some silky substance were growing upon it.

Right then, Gertrude shoved a black cloth into Scooter's mouth while Vivy tied a thin rope around his head to keep the gag in place.

"You're much more pleasant when you're quiet," Vivy said sweetly. "Just like the rest of your brothers and sisters. We've never had more trouble than the day we kidnapped them. They fought and bit and kicked. Some even cried for your mother. But we still managed to capture them. Isn't that right, sisters?"

The other two Gubble sisters cocked their heads back and laughed.

Witches, Scooter realized. *I should have known.*

Scooter leaned over to try and bite Gertrude's arm, but Vivy and Gertrude grabbed his head and held it still before he could strike. Issa lifted her dress and removed the small club which had been held in place by her garter stocking. She bent down over Scooter, who squirmed violently.

"Now there, young man, think of it this way—you'll get to be with your brothers and sisters soon. Doesn't that sound nice? Of course, we haven't yet found your twin sister, but, don't worry, we will."

Without hesitation, Issa thumped Scooter's head with the club and watched as his eyes rolled back in his head. A slight trickle of blood ran through his hair and down his neck, and Issa wiped it away with her thumb. She lifted her thumb to her lips and tasted the blood with her tongue.

"Shall we go back to town and look for his sister? She must be nearby. They're never far apart, and I hate to leave one behind," Gertrude proposed.

"We haven't the time right now," Issa replied. "We need to put these two with the rest of them, and then we can see how much time remains before—"

Right then, Stokely ran out of the darkness and rammed her shoulder into Issa's stomach. Issa tumbled backwards through the air and landed in the shadows. Before the other two sisters could react, Stokely grabbed them by the hair and slammed their heads together. They screamed in pain as Stokely fell to her knees next to her brother.

"Scooter, quick! Come on!" she pleaded.

But Scooter lay as still as a corpse.

The sisters pulled themselves up from the ground and stood like ferocious monsters, huffing in anger.

"You stupid girl!" Issa growled. "I'll get you if it's the last thing I ever do!"

Issa lurched forward, but Stokely dove out of the way and front-rolled to her feet.

"Get her!" Issa commanded.

Gertrude blocked Stokely's path. When Stokely turned around, Vivy caught her and slammed her against the stone wall. Vivy and Gertrude spread their arms as they closed in on the girl like wolves cornering their prey. Issa soon joined them, her hair ruffled from the tumble she had taken.

"You don't know what you're doing. What you're trying to stop, should not be stopped," Vivy threatened. "The Black Candle has already been lit, and Malivar will be here soon."

Stokely sensed something strangely alluring in the woman's voice.

"Come quietly, and it will be easier for you. Trust us,"

Gertrude encouraged.

Stokely looked around at the three Gubble sisters closing in on her. She knew she had no other choice. She dropped her hands by her side and hung her head in surrender.

"Alright," she conceded. "I'll go with you."

"You're smarter than the other children," Gertrude said. "I wish all of them had been as easily persuaded."

"Just take a sip of the brew, darling, and we'll take care of the rest," Vivy instructed with a smile. "It will all be over soon."

Issa lifted a glass vial which hung on a string around her neck. She unscrewed the black top of the tiny container, and offered it to Stokely, who took it into her trembling hands.

"Drink deep, lovely girl," Issa encouraged. "This is the last serving of our brew for this October, so don't let any go to waste."

Stokely stared down at the glass vial. The scent of the brew was more desirable than anything she could have imagined.

Stokely slowly lifted the vial to her lips. The Gubble sisters watched with great anticipation as the girl emptied the brew into her mouth, and looked up at the sisters with a satisfied smile.

"Any moment now, you'll drift off to a world of dreams," Gertrude said. "Did you like the taste? It's made of the rarest and sweetest ingredients."

Stokely swayed back and forth with her hand over her stomach, as if she were about to fall over.

"Get a sack ready," Issa commanded Vivy. "She's

almost in slumber."

But before Vivy could prepare the extra sack, Stokely spewed the liquid into Issa's eyes and sprinted away into the darkness.

Stokely felt her way along the walls of the tunnels, following the path that she hoped led back toward Town Square. In front of her, a stream of light poured down into the tunnels from some unseen source above. Stokely ran toward the light.

Arriving at a staircase which led up towards the source of the light, she climbed towards the open cellar door. After she lifted herself through the door, she immediately realized where she was. The intoxicating scent of chocolate cakes, vanilla puffs, and cinnamon buns filled the room.

Stokely stood behind the counter of Gubbles' Goodies. The cauldron of the brew lay tipped on its side, and the liquid had spread over the floor. She quickly ran around the counter and out the door into Town Square.

Not a soul stirred in town. No Hobbler dared roam the streets of Hobble on such a wicked night.

"Help!" Stokely cried out. "Someone please help me! The Gubbles have taken my brother!"

Right then, a loud thud sounded behind her.

Stokely wheeled around to see a tall, brown-haired boy, dressed in what looked like a Hallows Eve costume, staring back at her with deep, stormy eyes.

It was the stable boy from the Candletin Inn.

Moony Jarman.

END OF BOOK THREE

DARE TO UNLOCK THE MYSTERIES.
READ ALL FOUR BOOKS TO SOLVE THE VANISHING

BOOK 1:
THE
TIME CRYSTAL

BOOK 2:
THE
HERMIT'S MANSION

BOOK 3:
THE
WATCHTOWER SECRET

BOOK 4:
THE
PROTECTOR'S EMERALD

Become a citizen of Hobble!

Visit

www.theoctobers.com

to receive your citizenship papers and
enter the OCTOBERS contests!

MOONSUNG
presents

FOR UPCOMING TITLES, VISIT:

WWW.MOONSUNGBOOKS.COM

Author websites:

J.H. Reynolds: www.moonsungbooks.com

Craig Cunningham: www.craigcunningham.blog.com

Made in the USA
Charleston, SC
12 October 2011